Dancing
on the Edge

HAN NOLAN

Dancing on the Edge

PUFFIN BOOKS

PUFFIN BOOKS
Published by the Penguin Group
Penguin Putnam Books for Young Readers,
345 Hudson Street, New York, New York 10014, U.S.A.
Penguin Books Ltd, 27 Wrights Lane, London W8 5TZ, England
Penguin Books Australia Ltd, Ringwood, Victoria, Australia
Penguin Books Canada Ltd,
10 Alcorn Avenue, Toronto, Ontario, Canada M4V 3B2
Penguin Books (N.Z.) Ltd, 182-190 Wairau Road, Auckland 10, New Zealand

Penguin Books Ltd,
Registered Offices: Harmondsworth, Middlesex, England

First published in the United States of America
by Harcourt Brace & Company, 1997
Published by Puffin Books,
a member of Penguin Putnam Books for Young Readers, 1999

10 9 8 7 6 5 4 3 2 1

Library of Congress Cataloging-in-Publication Data
Nolan, Han.
Dancing on the edge/Han Nolan.
p.   cm.
Summary: A young girl from a dysfunctional family creates for herself an
alternative world that nearly results in her death but that ultimately leads her
to reality.
ISBN 0-15-201648-1
[1. Family problems—Fiction.   2. Supernatural—Fiction.]   I. Title.
PZ7.N6783Dan   1997
[Fic]—dc 21   96-52152

Poetry excerpts reprinted by permission of the publishers and the Trustees of
Amherst College from THE POEMS OF EMILY DICKINSON, Thomas H.
Johnson, ed., Cambridge, Mass.: The Belknap Press of Harvard University
Press. Copyright © 1951, 1955, 1979, 1983 by the President and Fellows of
Harvard College.

Excerpts from Poem #288 also reprinted by permission of Little, Brown and
Company.

Printed in the United States of America

Reprinted by arrangement with Penguin Putnam Inc.

For Brian,
Adrienne, and Rachael
My truest, realest loves

Part 1

"I'm Nobody! Who are you?"

—EMILY DICKINSON

Chapter 1

GIGI SAID my guardian angel must have been watching over me real good when I was born. Maybe so, but I wish the angel had watched over me less and seen to Mama more. I never liked hearing about how I came into this world anyway. It didn't seem natural, a live baby coming out of the body of a dead woman. Gigi said it was the greatest miracle ever to come down the pike.

"That's how come we call you Miracle," she told me for the millionth time when I was ten, after she had recited the whole story. She and Dane, my daddy, were setting up the card table for the séance we were going to have with Aunt Casey and Uncle Toole that night.

"And there's no need hanging your head like there's something to be ashamed of, you hear? Being pulled live from your mama's twisted body like that was an omen, a portent of great things to come, isn't that right, Dane?" She slid the Ouija board out of the box and set it on the card table. Dane didn't answer her, and she could tell by the way he studied the floorboards, his brows bunched up in fierce concentration, that he was too busy with his own important thoughts to bother with anything we might have to say. Gigi just kept right on talking anyway.

"She'll be something great one of these days," she said, nodding, her silver-streaked bun bobbling on top of her head. "You mark my words, I'll discover her special talent and I'll—"

"Need anything else done, Mama?" Dane asked, cutting her off. He never liked having to take time out from his thinking to do anything. I liked to think a lot, too, and it often got me in trouble with the teachers at school who accused me of daydreaming, so I understood. Gigi did, too, most of the time. She told him we'd do just fine without him and for him to go on back down to his room, and she'd send me down later with a tray of sweet tea and sandwiches for him.

Dane lit up a cigarette and blew the first puff at the ceiling. I watched his eyes follow the swirl of smoke. Then I saw them narrow into little slits, and he stayed like that a minute or two, squinting at the ceiling, lost in thought again. I studied him, with his long, long body and his shoulders hunched forward as if he'd been wounded in the chest, and I wanted to do something—dance, or show him my report card with all the A's again—something that would lift him up, smooth out the furrows in his face, and bring light to the dull glances he gave me. I touched his hand and it startled him. He looked down, scowling at first, and then seeing it was just me, his scowl disappeared and he blinked. Then, without a word he turned and shuffled away, his

4

slippers flapping at his heels and his bathrobe sash dragging behind him like a tail.

To look at him you wouldn't think my daddy ever did a lick of work, always in that robe and slippers with the mashed-down heels, but he was a writer, a prodigy. He had his first novel published when he was just thirteen, and Gigi always said that right away he was a literary sensation, the great Dane McCloy! I had a copy of his book on my shelf, and inside the book, below the title, Dane had written to me, "For Miracle, with love, Dane McCloy." It was my own special copy, and I told Dane that I loved it even though I had only read the last page. It was the first book I'd ever owned that didn't end with "And they lived happily ever after."

He wrote his next book when he was fifteen and the next at seventeen, the same year he married Mama, who was four months pregnant with me. Gigi always said that four is a sacred and holy number. She said all numbers are important because they contain all things in the natural and spiritual world, but I didn't like the number four because four and a half months after Mama married Dane, she got run over by an ambulance speeding to the scene of an accident. They pulled over and put Mama on a stretcher and kept her alive long enough to pick up the real accident victims, but by the time they wheeled her into the hospital she was dead. Then, of course, came the part where they realized the woman they ran over was pregnant and not fat and even though I should have been dead, too, by that time, they cut Mama open and out I came, full of portents and omens—a miracle.

Yes, I had heard the story many times, but it was

hearing it that night, six years ago, that stands out in my mind. That was the night I learned that portents and omens could mean the foretelling of something bad as well as something good.

It was the night of the séance with Aunt Casey and Uncle Toole. For once I was going to get to stay up and participate, maybe even talk to Mama if Aunt Casey would let me. Sissy, my mama, was Aunt Casey's younger sister, and Dane said when the two of them connected on the Ouija board, there was no getting a word in edgewise, which I could imagine to be true because Aunt Casey always had to give her opinion about everything.

I was so excited about the séance, I couldn't stay away from the Ouija board, and all afternoon I kept pestering Gigi. I wanted her to explain everything to me so I'd look professional and Aunt Casey wouldn't make fun of me. Gigi was patient with me for a while. She explained about the pointed wooden thing with the nail poking down in the middle. "This is called a planchette," she said. "Now you place your fingertips on one side like so, and then I place mine on the other. Now, not so heavy. Lightly, lightly, like you're resting them on marshmallows. Good. Now tonight, if we get us a spirit, this planchette will start moving. And you don't push it, hear? Your fingers stay soft, let them just go along for the ride." Gigi pushed the planchette across the board and watched my fingers. I held them so they were just barely touching the wooden edge.

"Good. Now the planchette will move over the alphabet or over to the word *yes* or *no*, or *good* or *bad*, or use the numbers. See, it can use any part of the board."

"And that will be the spirit talking to us?" I asked. "That will be Mama talking?"

"That's right, baby doll." She left me then to go finish up her load of laundry in the basement. I stayed at the table, playing Ouija with my Barbie doll, and thought about all the questions I was going to ask Mama, the same questions I had asked her every night since I could remember. "Where are you, Mama?" I always began, lying in my bed and staring up into the darkness, feeling her silence. "Where is the spirit world? Is it just like heaven? Are you happy? Do you know who I am? Do you know what I look like? They say I'm small for my age and way too skinny, and I feel small, Mama, like the smallest seed, so far away from you. I'm taking good care of Dane. Do you know that? Are you proud of me for looking after Dane?"

Finally, Gigi said I had fiddled enough with the board and I was getting too much body heat on the planchette. She told me to leave it alone and find myself something else to do for the next hour.

I slipped Dane's *Bob Dylan's Greatest Hits* tape into my tape player and sang and danced all over the living room furniture. I was teetering on the arm of the sofa, trying to do an arabesque, when Aunt Casey came hipswaying into the room. She stopped halfway across, looked at me with her mean eyeliner eyes, and said, "Miracle, does your grandmama know you're out here busting up her furniture?"

"Sure she does," I lied. "I'm going to be a great prodigy someday, and I need to practice. Gigi says so."

I did a flip off the armrest and landed standing with both feet on the seat cushion. I held out my arms and bowed to her.

"Big hoo-hoo to you," she said. "You aren't any kind of prodigy. It's not hereditary. As a matter of fact, it's a freak accident. Your daddy's a freak. You just look it up in the dictionary. A prodigy is something abnormal or monstrous."

I jumped off the sofa. "I'm not listening to you," I said, covering my ears. She always had something mean to say about Dane, or me, or both of us. I think it riled her good that he was famous, a child prodigy, as if somehow his being one took something away from her.

Just seeing her and Uncle Toole coming up the walk could make my stomach cringe: Aunt Casey, tall and slim and stiff-legged in her too-high heels, and Uncle Toole a head shorter and looking tough, just daring anyone to notice a difference in their heights. And I knew at the very least Aunt Casey would be looking at me all night, the way she always did, as if it hurt her face, as if it were painful.

I told Gigi once that I didn't know why they had to be dropping by all the time as if they were neighbors. They lived two whole towns away. They weren't really even family anymore. "Casey's just Dane's ex–sister-in-law," I said, and then added, "It's true, Dane told me so," when I caught the way Gigi studied me, as if she were making some decision about what she wanted to say to me. She appeared worried, then frightened, her pink jowly face suddenly pale, almost gray, and then with a sweep of her hand in front of her face, her expression changed, her color returned, and she smiled and said in a voice that sounded flat and rehearsed, "With Sissy gone, we're the only family Casey has. She may be an in-law to me and Dane, but she's your aunt, so you be nice to her." Then Gigi closed her eyes and started humming, her signal that the conversation had ended; she had gone into a trance.

I wanted to ask her more about Aunt Casey, and lots more about Mama. I always wanted to ask more, but she never let me. Gigi didn't like me asking a lot of questions. She said my questions upset the karmic balance, and I knew this was so, because even though I didn't know what karmic balance meant, I could tell how upset my questions made her.

So I tried to be nice to Aunt Casey, but the best I could do was to just stay out of her way.

The night of the séance, I grabbed my Barbie doll off the card table and flopped down on the floor with it. I tried to pretend Aunt Casey wasn't in the room with me. Then "Just Like a Woman" started playing, and Aunt Casey turned up the volume.

"I love this song," she said, mashing her cigarette into the brickwork and then flicking the dead butt into the fireplace. She closed her eyes and leaned back against the wall in a way that made her narrow hips poke out of her spandex pants like big old cow bones. Her face wore a peaceful, happy expression for a change, and her hair was crammed beneath a scarf with fat pink sponge curlers poking out every which way. I looked at her and then at my Barbie doll with its plastic face, narrow waist, and large bust. They looked alike. I tossed the doll over my shoulder. Uncle Toole had just come into the room and the doll landed at his feet.

"See, sugar, I told you women just threw themselves at me."

"You see me laughing, Toole Dawsey?" Aunt Casey pushed off the wall and set her hands on her hip bones. The two of them were always either fighting or acting all lovey-dovey with each other, and being around them either way just gave me the hives. I jumped to my feet, thinking I'd go find Dane, but then Uncle Toole stretched his hairy arms out to me and scooped me up, tossing me onto his shoulder. I don't know why but he always had to pick me up and turn me upside down when he saw me. It hurt because he did it so fast and handled me like one of the crates he lifted and loaded all day. Even if it didn't hurt, I wouldn't have liked it because he scared me. He was big-muscled and square all over, with a snarly, growly sounding voice and a scar on his forehead that looked as if the long jagged edge of a piece of glass had cut into him.

"Miracle, you're getting so heavy I might drop you," he said, loosening his grip around my ankles some. "Oops! Oops! Watch out." He lowered me to the ground on my head, let go, and I did a somersault and scooted out of his way.

Gigi rattled in with the tray of iced tea and glasses. "Is everybody ready?" she asked.

Aunt Casey turned off my tape player and took her seat at the table. The rest of us joined her, and then wouldn't you know it, Toole had to point me out.

"Whoa, what's going on here? Why ain't the baby toddling on off to bed? Are we having us a see-ance or a romper room here?" He gave us all his squinted-up, suspicious look, the one he always gave people whenever he felt they knew something he didn't know and they weren't saying what.

I looked to Gigi and she squinched her nose up at me. I smiled back.

"Dane is working," Gigi said, "and we need a fourth, and anyway, it's high time we introduced Miracle to some of her ancestors."

"I want to talk to Mama," I said, so excited I was ready to pee in my pants.

Uncle Toole arched back in his chair and puffed out his chest. "Shoot," he said, shaking his square head and giving me a nasty look.

Aunt Casey pulled the two cigarettes she had just lit out of her mouth and handed one to Uncle Toole. "Don't be rude to the child," she said, blowing her smoke over my head.

Uncle Toole looked at the pink lipstick around the tip of the cigarette. Pink, the color symbol for all things female, as Gigi would say. He took a drag and blew the smoke out at me with a long low burp.

"Toole!" Gigi and Aunt Casey said at the same time.

"Shoot, let's just do it, okay?" he said, pulling forward in his seat and resting his wide, hairy hands on the edge of the Ouija board.

Gigi lit three of the candles that hung from a chandelier over the table and turned out the lights.

We all sat with our hands placed before us on the table and waited for a signal from Gigi. She had closed her eyes and was taking deep breaths through her nose and letting them out through the O she made with her lips. The candles flickered above us, casting dancing shadows in the room and on our faces. I looked at the

11

three people sitting with me and they didn't look like themselves at all. Gigi's long nose looked longer and waxy, like Silly Putty, her loose-skinned face all lumpy, and the fat bun on the top of her head looked like a big old mud pie. Aunt Casey's head with the curlers made her look like a space creature, and the long strokes of eyeliner extending beyond the outer corners of her own eyes made her look evil, her green cat eyes squinting and blinking like sinister signals. And Uncle Toole's scar had gone a dark, deep red, as if his blood were pulsating through all that dead tissue, bringing it to life.

Gigi whispered, "I want you all to see Sissy. Close your eyes and concentrate. See her. See her."

I heard Aunt Casey whisper, "Yes."

"See her. Feel her near," Gigi said.

I closed my eyes and thought of the picture of Mama Dane had on top of his writing desk. She was swinging on a giant iron gate and smiling for the camera, but to me she looked sad, the smile on her lips not reaching her eyes. I wondered if she knew then she was going to die young. I wondered if people knew deep down when they were going to die.

Gigi began to hum, and we all placed our fingertips on the planchette.

We sat listening to the low tone of her hum for a few minutes, and then I saw Gigi's body jerk sideways. "Who's there?" she asked.

The planchette moved. I felt goose bumps rise up on my arms, and my bottom began to itch. The planchette moved again, and it felt as if the guide piece were simply floating beneath my fingertips. I knew I wasn't making it move. I looked at Uncle Toole. His eyes were closed. So were Aunt Casey's and Gigi's. The planchette stopped moving and they opened their eyes. The nail was pointing at the letter R.

"Rasmus, is that you?" Gigi asked.

We started moving again, faster. The nail pointed to the word *yes*.

"We want to talk to Sissy. Is she there?"

The planchette moved away from the *yes* and then slid back.

I started chewing on my lip. I wanted to talk to her. I wanted to talk to Mama.

"Sissy, your baby's here. Your little girl. Your Miracle."

I inched forward in my seat and both Aunt Casey and Uncle Toole shushed me.

The planchette started moving again, quickly, smoothly, almost floating over the surface of the board. It slid to the *T*, then the *R*, then *O-U-B-L-E*.

"What kind of trouble?" Gigi asked.

Again the planchette was moving, and I could feel my fingers trembling. I had chewed a sore into my lip, and I worked at it and watched the planchette float over to the *D*, then to *A-N-E*.

Trouble for Dane, I thought. I began to relax. People were always saying that. "What's the trouble with Dane?" they'd ask. "Where's his next book?" they'd wonder. "Wasn't that novel he wrote nine years ago supposed to be part of a trilogy?" Dane had been having trouble with his writing ever since Mama died and I was born.

"What trouble, Sissy?" Gigi asked.

I looked at Gigi. I wanted to talk. When was she going to let me talk?

Again the planchette spelled out Dane but then continued to the G and then to O and then it paused and, just when I thought the message was over, it moved again to the N and then to E.

"Gone?" Gigi asked. "Dane gone?"

The planchette moved slowly to the *yes.*

"Dane gone?" Aunt Casey whispered. "When?" She looked up at Gigi. "Ask Sissy when."

The planchette moved one more time and spelled out *N-O-W.*

Chapter 2

WE SCRAMBLED OVER each other trying to be the first one down the steps to Dane's room in the basement. We were in such a hurry that no one thought to turn on any lights, and I heard Uncle Toole bumping down the steps on his bottom. He was shouting *Whoa! Whoa!* on his way down, but his cowboy boots must have been digging into nothing because he didn't stop till he hit bottom. Then in the hallway, we stumbled all over each other again, feeling our way along the stone walls to Dane's door. I got there first and flung open the door shouting, "Dane! Dane, we're here!"

Uncle Toole grabbed me and held me back.

"Holy sh—," he said.

We all stood together in a breathless clump, bedazzled by the lights of Dane's candle bottles. They were everywhere—on his shelves, on his desk, lining the edges of the window casements, and covering the floor like a flaming blanket.

"What is this?" Aunt Casey asked, twisting to see Gigi.

I answered her, whispering with pride. "Dane's candle bottles. He likes to plug all his empty wine bottles with candles and then we light them, in ceremony."

"In ceremony of what?" Aunt Casey's voice was harsh.

"Casey, leave it," Gigi said.

"But where's Dane?" I asked, stepping into the room. Uncle Toole caught me by the shoulders and pulled me back.

"He ain't in here, that's for sure," he said.

Then Gigi brushed past us, her purple séance robe swinging into the bottles, making us all gasp.

Aunt Casey said, "Lord, Gigi, you want to go up in flames? Watch that robe."

Gigi didn't hear her. She glided around the bottles, moving toward Dane's writing desk. Then she stopped and held up both her arms the way she did when calling on the dead spirits. We knew she had come upon something.

"Would you look?" she said. "What in the world?"

We all crept into the room, looking for what Gigi saw.

"His clothes!" She pointed to a heap on the floor. "If that isn't the strangest thing. Look at the way they're setting, like he was just in them a second ago."

It *was* strange. We all agreed on that. Dane's uniform: his sweats, his bathrobe, his underwear, his slippers with the backs mashed down, lay on the floor in the midst of the candles, looking as if his body had just

16

melted clear out of them and all that was left was the heap of clothes.

Then Gigi cried out, "He's melted," and I heard this and knew it was so.

"Woman, you're out of your head," Uncle Toole said. "People don't melt."

"The witch in the *Wizard of Oz* did," I said, imagining Dane calling out for help and nobody hearing him. My legs began to shake.

Gigi leaned forward and picked up two of the bottles and held them over her head and cried out again. "Dane! Dane!"

I cried out, too, but Uncle Toole grabbed my shoulders again and tried to lead me back out of the room. "This ain't nothing for a ten-year-old to see."

"But I want to. What's wrong? What's happened? Why did he melt?" I twisted away from him, my shoulders aching from the strong pressure of his squeezing fingers.

"He didn't melt," Uncle Toole said. "See what you started, Gigi?"

Gigi didn't answer. She was on her knees, surrounded by the candle bottles, swaying in circles and moaning.

I darted around the bottles and joined Gigi on the floor, and Uncle Toole stood behind us cussing while Aunt Casey yelled at him to shut up.

Gigi and I stayed on our knees swaying for a long time. I don't know when Aunt Casey and Uncle Toole left because I had to concentrate on being just like Gigi. I kept waiting for Dane to reappear, because it seemed

17

to me that's why we stayed down there on the floor with our arms crossed over our chests moaning to the spirits. I thought Gigi was trying to conjure him up, but he never came back. The candles burned down, and I grew tired. I climbed up on Dane's bed and fell asleep, my face buried in my daddy's bathrobe.

PEOPLE IN OUR TOWN didn't like hearing about how Dane melted. It was as if it were some kind of threat to them, as if they could melt any minute themselves —from the sun, a heated room, a candlelit dinner. Gigi said it wasn't worth trying to explain to them that not just anyone could melt like that.

"Our specialness scares them, baby, that's why we've got to move," she said to me one day when I came home from school and found her and Aunt Casey packing up the living room.

And it was true what she said about us scaring people. Even the police and the newspaper reporters who swarmed around the house and the yard were timid around us. They suspected Gigi of foul play, that's what the newspapers said at first: MOTHER OF PRODIGY SUSPECTED OF FOUL PLAY. Then when they realized that everything he owned and wore was still in the house, that wherever he was, he was naked, they suspected both murder and suicide and had the pond in back of our house dredged.

About a week after the disappearance, as they were calling it, the papers got ahold of our theory about him melting and wrote a long article about Gigi and her practicing the black arts. The night after that came out, Gigi came creeping into my room in the middle of the night, her slingshot in one hand and her sack of marbles in the other.

I sat up in bed. "What's going on?" I asked.

"Go back to sleep, baby. I just got to deal with some adults who ought to know better."

"What?" I rose on my knees and looked out my window. I could see something moving out there, dark shadowlike figures.

"Your window's the best chance I've got of getting a good shot."

"Who are they?" I asked. "What's that they're doing?"

"Shh, I've got to get out on your roof without them noticing me. Here, you can hand me my sack once I'm out."

Gigi handed me the marbles and silently lifted my window. Someone outside lit a torch and I ducked, thinking they could see us, but Gigi kept on moving through the window and out onto the roof, as easily as a black cat in satin slippers. She had always been light on her feet even though she was heavy, her movements graceful, careful.

I could see the figures real well now. Two of them held torches while three others sprinkled something along the edge of our lawn.

"Are they spooks?" I whispered through the window, remembering how some of the kids at school had said our house was full of them.

Gigi turned her head to me and put her finger up to her mouth. "Shh. They're just people up to no good." She signaled for me to hand her the marbles.

I passed the sack through the window and held my

breath. So far no one had noticed her. Gigi selected her marble, placed it in the sling, and aimed. I knew it would hit its mark as soon as she drew back the sling. Dane always said Gigi had a dead-straight aim. She let go of the sling and in a flash one of the bodies out there, a woman's, let out a scream, and dropped to her knees.

"I've been shot! Lord, Ray, I've been shot, right between the eyes," she howled. "I'm gonna die! I'm gonna die!"

The others stopped what they were doing and stood over the woman on the ground.

Gigi took aim again and shot another marble through the air.

"Dang!" came a man's voice. He grabbed his head and fell on his knees. "They're shooting at us! I've been shot in the back of the head."

Another voice said, "I didn't hear anything."

"It's that voodoo stuff," the man hit with the second marble said. "Now, let's get out of here. The bullet's probably lodged in my brain, set to explode any minute." He trotted beside the others, keeping low, as they lugged the fainted woman out to the truck.

Gigi didn't say anything until they drove out of sight. Then she stood up on the roof and let out a wolf howl.

I stood next to the window clapping, proud to be granddaughter to such a fine person as my Gigi.

The next day, I came home to find Gigi and Aunt Casey packing and saying we had to leave Alabama.

"But didn't we win?" I asked. "Didn't they run off?"

I looked at both of them. Aunt Casey's eyes red. I wondered why she had been crying.

"It wasn't about winning, sugar pie," Gigi said, her back to me. She leaned over her table of glass figurines and wrapped one of them for packing. "I just didn't want them trespassing on my property. But it's time we move on now, with Dane melted and people around here so excited."

"But what if Dane comes back? We wouldn't be here. He could come looking for us and we wouldn't be here!"

Gigi shook her head and turned around, but she still didn't look at me. She looked at Aunt Casey, who held her head down, staring at her red-painted toenails, red, the color of rage.

"I can't raise you up around this. You need an accepting environment. You're special, aren't you, sugar pie?" She looked at me then and said, "Weren't you born from the body of a dead woman?"

I shook my head. "I'd better go pack," I said, rushing for the stairs and keeping my head turned away so they couldn't see my face.

"Casey will bring you some boxes," Gigi called after me.

I ran to my room and closed the door. I didn't want to hear their voices. I didn't want to hear the story about Mama and my miracle birth. Ever since Dane melted I'd become afraid of that story, as if my being born from a dead woman had something to do with his melting. They were the same kind of thing to me. Thinking of either one of them made my stomach squeeze up tight. They made me feel all wrong inside,

21

and there was something more to it—my birth and his melting—something I couldn't quite put my finger on. All I knew was that it had to do with me.

The way the kids avoided me at school told me they knew, and the teachers who stood together and whispered about me knew, too. There was some big, wrong thing about me, and everybody knew what it was, except me. I wanted to run up to Gigi and ask, "What is it? Why don't you see me anymore? Why are you always in your room now, or out? Why aren't you home when I come home from school? What did I do?" But I knew I couldn't ask those kinds of questions. I knew it would upset the karmic balance. Instead, I took to wearing Dane's bathrobe, a soft coat of armor protecting me, wrapping me in its warm smells of cigarettes, wine, and musty old books—Dane's smell.

I heard Aunt Casey on the stairs, banging the wall with the moving boxes. She kicked at my door, and I let her in.

"Here you go, Miracle," she said, all out of breath. She dropped the boxes on the floor and leaned against the door frame.

I picked up a box. "Thanks."

"No sweat. How about I help you with some of this stuff?" She hip-swayed over to my chest of drawers and picked up my Barbie doll. "It shouldn't take long, you don't have half of nothing. Just books." She ran her hand along the top row of my bookshelf, looking like some lone wanderer dragging a stick along a picket fence. She tossed my Barbie into the box I was holding. "Shoot, you don't even have a Ken doll. What's a Barbie without a Ken? Huh? What's a Barbie all by herself?"

I brought my box over to the bookshelf. "I don't like Ken. He doesn't have real hair. It's plastic painted hair."

Aunt Casey laughed, and I saw bits of red lipstick stuck on her teeth. "Now look at these books. Dane must have picked these out, all this Shakespeare—*Hamlet* and *Macbeth*, *A Midsummer Night's Dream*. Hasn't he ever heard of Nancy Drew?"

"Who?" I asked.

Aunt Casey dragged her own box over to the shelves and started pulling out my books and stacking them in the boxes.

"I bet you don't get along too well at that school of yours, reading Shakespeare and listening to old-timey Bob Dylan."

"Dane loves Bob Dylan," I said.

"He sounds constipated," said Aunt Casey.

We each filled our boxes without saying anything more, and then when Aunt Casey handed me my purple spiritual clothes from out of my closet, the ones Gigi had picked out for me, for when the color of my aura needed changing, I said, "No one likes me at this school. I'm glad we're moving."

Aunt Casey stopped handing me the clothes and squatted in front of me. "You're special, that's all. You're different. I'm sorry what I said before about Nancy Drew." She patted my shoulder, something Aunt Casey had never done before. "Shoot, they're just jealous, I bet."

I shook my head. "They call me names and throw stuff at me. They say bad things about Dane and me."

Aunt Casey looked into my face, the rims of her round eyes still red. "What kinds of stuff, sugar?"

"Mean stuff about how he always looks so creepy when he drives into town, like he's drunk. They say he's crazy. He talks to himself all the time and never answers anyone's questions. And they say that sometimes he just walks into a store, picks out what he wants, and right in front of everyone, walks back out again without paying. They say he belongs in jail."

"Jail! Nonsense! You know, honey, that's just Dane. He forgets to shave, to wash, to brush his teeth. He's always been like that."

"They're saying now we're all crazy, and we got spooks living with us."

"Spooks? Who ever heard of such nonsense? Really!"

"They're even calling *me* a spook." I said, telling her the worst of it, the part that troubled me the most, because I was starting to believe it, starting to feel like a spook.

Aunt Casey stood back up. "Well, never you mind them. I'm glad you're moving. I am. I just wish I were coming with you."

"You and Uncle Toole aren't coming?" I hitched up my shoulder and turned away from her. Even if I didn't like them much, I knew it couldn't be a good thing losing them so soon after losing Dane.

"Hah!" Aunt Casey said, coming around to face me. "Your uncle Toole can stay right here, but maybe I'll come. That would serve Mr. Hot Pants right."

"You and Uncle Toole have another fight? Is that why you've been crying?" I studied her face, so thin and pinched, and I noticed even with her pain, she looked pretty. Her skin was smooth and her green eyes seemed greener, bigger.

"I shouldn't have been crying. Not over him, that . . . that roving eyeball! Trotting after that Delphinnia woman. She's got nothing special, besides her name. But I fixed Toole good—shaved off his eyebrows and cut his eyelashes. He was too drunk and passed out to notice. Went to work today wearing ladies' sunglasses." Aunt Casey laughed, but there were tears coming out of her eyes and the tip of her nose had turned red.

She wiped her eyes and shook her head. "Of course, I've got my business. I guess I couldn't exactly leave my beauty business, all my clients."

She went over to my chest of drawers and stared at herself in the mirror, patting her hair and fluffing it up at the top. She had dyed it black. Last time I saw her, it was red. She changed hair color as often as most people changed their socks, and it made her hair appear brittle and stiff and oversprayed.

"No, I can't leave my clients," she said. "At least they need me." She turned around. "But hey, how about I give you a new do before you go, huh? No charge. Wouldn't you like a haircut, to celebrate the new you in a new town?"

I shrugged. "Okay, I guess so."

Aunt Casey ran to the door. "I'll only be a minute. I've got a kit in my purse. This will perk us up, won't it? Now you be thinking how you want it, I'll be right back."

She left the room and I stared at the door, thinking about Aunt Casey and her beauty salon. She owned it and managed it, and even had a wig-fitting business in her home where she fitted wigs for cancer patients. It was the only nice thing I'd ever known her to do until that day when she offered to cut my hair for me.

I wandered over to my chest of drawers and stared down at the red fingernail polish I'd painted on my nails. I had painted them the day of the séance so Mama wouldn't see the dirt underneath, but already the polish had chipped down to little flecks in the center of each nail. I made fists with my hands so I couldn't see the nails and took a deep breath. I wanted to look at myself in the mirror, but lately, every time I tried, a queer, queasy-hot feeling came over me. I couldn't look.

It used to be, before Dane melted, that whenever I saw myself, it was a surprise, a shock. I had spent so many hours studying Mama's face in the picture Dane had on his writing desk that I expected to see her looking back at me in the mirror. I expected her freckles and brown, almond-shaped eyes, but my eyes were round and blue, and my face long and Elmer's-Glue white, not one freckle. Mine was the pale, blank stare of a stranger. But now when I looked in the mirror, there was a new surprise, a new expectation, and it scared me more than anything. Because now, I didn't expect to see my reflection at all.

Chapter 3

AUNT CASEY cut my hair in the bathroom.

"You sit right there on the toilet," she said. "You're getting so tall I can't have you standing anymore. Anyway, I do some of my best work on the toilet."

"You sound like Uncle Toole," I said, sitting on the seat with my back to her.

"That just shows you, don't marry a man unless you like the way he talks. Now, how are we going to cut your hair? How about bangs? You like bangs?"

"I want Dane's haircut," I said.

Aunt Casey leaned way over to get a look at my face. "That's a man's haircut, sugar."

"I know." I hung my head forward, staring into my lap. Dane wore his hair short, almost buzzed. He said it drove him crazy to feel hair on his neck or creeping down over his ears or on his forehead. Lately, mine had been driving me crazy, too. I was always feeling it on my shoulders or tickling my cheek. I found myself pulling at it in school when I was working or thinking or trying to fall off to sleep at night. I didn't want to feel it anymore. I didn't want to know it was there.

"Please could I have Dane's haircut, anyway?" I said, twisting my neck to see her.

Aunt Casey sighed and straightened back up. She sprayed my hair wet, combed it out, and started cutting.

"Look at you, wearing that ratty old bathrobe of his," she said, straightening my head. "Gigi says you've been wearing it every day. Ever since he melted. Said you're even wearing it to school. You must miss Dane awful, huh?"

I shrugged and played with the tie on the bathrobe. "He's my daddy," I said, hoping Aunt Casey couldn't tell, standing behind me, how much I really missed him. I didn't need her making fun of me.

Before Dane melted, I used to spend every day after school with him, down in his room. He called his room "The Cave," and it was long and narrow with walls made of stone. He used the candle bottles to light the room, and they flickered and cast shadows on the walls so that even in our own silence and stillness we had movement, we had something going on.

Most of the time Dane sat at his writing desk and either stared at his computer, occasionally tapping out words on his keyboard, or he read. I sat on his bed with my homework in my lap, taking my time with each subject so that I'd have a reason to stay down there with him.

Sometimes he'd say, "Listen to this," and he'd stand up and pace and read me a part of the story he was writing, the candle lights leaning and straining on the breath of his movement as he passed. I never understood what he read to me, and sometimes he didn't seem to be reading words at all, just sounds. Still, I listened and watched him pace from one end of the room to the other, six steps each direction, six, the number for creation, and I felt full and happy and complete.

Now, whenever I went down to the cave, I felt lost—sitting alone on his bed, listening for him, waiting, asking the floor, the walls, the candle bottles to let him come back. I didn't know how to bring him back. I didn't even know how to think about his melting. Should I cry? Gigi didn't cry. He didn't die, so we didn't have a funeral. We couldn't go looking for him, either. Where do you look for a melted person?

I thought about the candle bottles and how when his work was going really well, or he'd just sent his manuscript off to his editor, he would invite me into his cave for the candle bottle lighting ceremony. We'd set up all the bottles in different patterns on the floor of his room. Then we'd light the candles and sit together on his bed and watch them, and Dane would describe to me the really big celebration we'd have when he sold his new book. And I could see it all. Through the flames of the candle bottles, I could see the magic that shimmered in the room and spiced the air, the kind of magic that gets you believing in miracles.

AUNT CASEY CUT MY HAIR just like Dane's, swearing that Gigi would kill the both of us, but Gigi liked it. She said short hair looked very stylish and chic.

"We should have had your hair cut like that long ago," she said to me in the car on our way to Grandaddy Opal's home just outside of Atlanta, Georgia. "It sets you apart. It makes a statement. It says to the world, 'Look out, 'cause Miracle McCloy is on her way.' It was the same with your daddy. He had that special something. I knew it from the day he was born, but your grandaddy didn't believe it, not a bit. He said, 'Dane needs to learn a trade, needs to learn how to work with his hands and work hard.'" She said this with a gruff man's voice, imitating Grandaddy Opal. Gigi divorced him because of Dane.

"If it weren't for me, your daddy would have been working at a sawmill or something. But that nice Mrs. Lundy let us use her little beach house. Right on the water it was, too. I helped her contact her dead brother, Albert, you know. Some people know how to show their gratitude. I bought Dane a typewriter and fixed him tuna and tomato sandwiches and made sure no one bothered him so he could just write and write and write. But did he ever thank me?"

I glanced over at Gigi. She was gripping the steering wheel and making faces as if she were having a conversation in her head with somebody. I figured she was going back over the argument she and Dane had had just a few days before he melted. Anytime Dane got upset about his work not going well, the two of them ended up in a big fight. I could always see it coming. First, there'd be several days when he wouldn't have any work to read to me, then he'd start swearing at his computer, and finally he'd tell me to "run on along" because he needed to be alone. I hated it when he'd tell me to leave because I knew if I had worked it right, steered him away from his worries, he'd be back to writing, and he and Gigi wouldn't end up saying hurtful words to each other, words that scared me.

Sometimes I'd get him to read me his favorite story by a man named Kafka. I could never remember the name of it so I'd say to him, "Read me that story about the man who turned into a cockroach." If I could convince him to read it, in no time he'd be back to thinking about his own story, and I could stay down in the cave with him, and he and Gigi wouldn't have their fight.

In their last argument, Dane blamed Gigi for messing up his life, which he did every time they fought. Then he said that Opal should have been the one raising me. He said if I were with Opal, I would have turned out normal, and that Gigi wasn't fit to raise a child and never had been.

I could tell by the way Gigi's mouth twisted down that he had hurt her to the core. She couldn't even think up a good comeback. She waited until he left the room before she said, "I must have done something right, Mr. Prodigy."

Gigi turned off the highway onto a road of fast-food restaurants and we poked along, stopping every minute at the red lights.

I leaned my head against the car window and tried to forget about Dane. I thought about Aunt Casey standing outside our house that morning, crying and waving good-bye. I hadn't expected her to carry on so about our leaving, and watching her gave me the uncomfortable feeling that she knew something about the move I didn't know. Her mascara and eyeliner streamed down her cheeks because she was allergic to everything waterproof, so there she stood, in a puddle of colors that had run off her face, waving a piece of toilet tissue and saying she'd visit when she could. I waved back and slunk down in my seat so that just my eyes were high enough to see out the window. I watched her dabbing at her eyes with the tissue and waving at us again. Then Gigi turned left out of the driveway and Aunt Casey was gone. It left me with a funny feeling, seeing her one second standing on the stoop waving, and the next second, without moving my eyes from her, seeing instead the bushes that ran along the edge of our property. I wondered if she was still there, or if she had disappeared. Maybe people existed only as long as you were seeing them, only as long as your mind could conjure them up. Maybe I existed only as long as someone was looking at me, or thinking about me. The rest of the time where was I? Who was I? I stared down at the dirty bits of bubble gum stuck to my fingers. I picked at the old gum and wondered, *What happens to a person when no one's thinking about her anymore?*

"Yes, I devoted my life to him. I made him what he is today," Gigi said, jumping back into my thoughts.

I looked over at her and saw her eyes watering and blinking.

"Now that Dane's melted, Gigi," I said, "where do you suppose he is?"

Gigi leaned forward, her large chest mashed against the steering wheel, and snatched a piece of toilet tissue out of the ashtray. She blew her nose and tossed the tissue onto the floor of the van. "Dane's where he's supposed to be, sugar pie. That's what it's all about, figuring where you ought to be and who you ought to be and then going and doing it."

"But where does melting take you? What place?"

"Oh, some other place, some other time," Gigi said, her right hand fiddling with the crystal she had hanging around her neck. "Wish I could tell you more, but that's the way melting works. It's a vague kind of thing, one of those mysteries of life scientists and spiritualists and other ists are always trying to figure out."

"Oh," I said, turning back to the window. I noticed people waving and smiling in the next car over, and I slid down in my seat. Anytime we left town in our van people stared or honked or pointed and waved—something. Gigi's van was a sight to behold. The outside had been painted a deep purple, of course—the most spiritual color—and on it were crystal balls and Ouija boards and tarot cards and hands and stars and a giant Egyptian-looking eye and the words "OPEN YOUR MIND AND TRAVEL BEYOND THE UNIVERSE!"

We turned into Grandaddy Opal's driveway, and I sat up straight, chewing on my lower lip. I didn't think moving in with Grandaddy Opal was such a good idea. I overheard Uncle Toole saying only someone as crazy as Gigi would go back and live with her ex-husband after fifteen years. Then Aunt Casey said they weren't going to be living as husband and wife. "Why, they don't even like each other," she said. "Haven't spoken to each other except lately, to say she needed to stay at his house awhile until she got back on her feet. But where else could she go? They were only renting that house of theirs, and the landlord told Gigi he'd read the article in the paper and he couldn't have people like

33

her renting his house anymore. Anyway, it's just going to be a kind of *arrangement*." And she emphasized the word making it sound like she meant to say derangement.

All I knew was that I didn't want to be there. Grandaddy Opal's name always came up in Gigi and Dane's fights, and so did mine, and they never sounded good together, my name and his—linked together when we didn't even know each other. Their angry words had always scared me, and I had the feeling now that Gigi planned to leave me there alone with him and go away.

Gigi got out of the car and said, "If you're waiting for Opal to come out and welcome us, you'll be sitting there forever. Now come on, we'll leave the U-Haul for now and just bring along our suitcases."

I waited until I saw Gigi lift her suitcase out of the back before climbing out of the van. Then I grabbed my bag and turned around to face Grandaddy Opal's house. It was small and squat and sat crowded in a neighborhood of other small, squat houses. Back where we used to live we didn't have neighbors, just fields and ponds. It was more conducive to Dane's work, Gigi had said. Gigi called Grandaddy Opal's house a bungalow. The shutters were all crooked, the way they are on haunted houses, and the porch slanted downhill so much I imagined people spilling out of the house, picking up momentum on the porch, and tumbling off the edge, missing the stairs completely.

I followed Gigi up the porch hill and into the house. As run-down as the outside was, the inside was tidy and white and smelled of new paint. Our house at home always smelled of Gigi's incense: of flowers and wet wood.

"We've got four rooms," Gigi said, setting her suitcases on the wood floor and spinning around, first right, then left, to ward off evil spirits. "This is the great room—living room, dining room, and whatever else—Opal doesn't use it." She took a bottle of rose water with a drop of liquid gold out of her pocket and poured some into her hands. Then she sprinkled it on the floor and furniture—for good luck and prosperity.

It was a large room. She had to use two handfuls of the rose water to charm the whole room. Grandaddy Opal had furnished it with a sectional sofa, an orange La-Z-Boy, and to one side a table and chair set. A double stack of *National Geographics* rising clear up to the ceiling stood next to the La-Z-Boy. They wobbled and threatened to topple over when we walked across the room.

"Then here . . ." She wandered out of the great room and I followed her. "This galley is the kitchen. Opal doesn't use this room much, either." Gigi did her spinning and sprinkling ritual again.

I followed her from the kitchen to the hallway. I could hear TV voices coming from behind the first closed door. "Opal's," Gigi said, rapping her knuckle on the closed door.

"Pipe down out there!" Grandaddy Opal growled.

"Bathroom," Gigi said, tapping the door on her other side. "And here"—she pushed open the last door—"is our room."

I took it all in at a glance. White walls, two cots, and

a table between them. I dropped my suitcase, spun around left then right, and ran to the little table. "Look! A TV!" I said. In all my ten and a half years of living I had never seen a television show. Dane said he didn't believe in television. I remember once Aunt Casey dragged him into her and Uncle Toole's bedroom, pointed at their TV set, and said, "See? Now you can't say you don't believe in TV. It exists, there it is. It's not like believing or not believing in God. You have to say you either accept TV or don't accept it; it's not a belief system, you know. And you call yourself a prodigy."

She acted real proud of that one. She always tried to catch Dane, trip him up somehow and make him look stupid. I believe the TV proof idea was one of her finest, because Dane stayed in a sulk all night long, and we had to go home early because he said his teeth hurt.

I switched our little set on and a gray-white light came up on the screen, nothing else, no sound, no picture.

"It's broken," I said to Gigi.

"It figures," she said.

WE'D BEEN IN Grandaddy Opal's house for a whole week and I still hadn't seen him. Then one night I heard him get up to go to the bathroom and I climbed out of my cot and waited in the doorway for him to come back out. I heard the toilet flush and the water run in the sink and my heart raced. Then the door opened and he jumped out in front of me like an ape springing down from a tree and shouted, "Boo!" I squealed and slammed the door in his hairy face.

I didn't see him to speak to until one day almost a

week later when Gigi left me at the house while she went looking for a real job. Ever since Dane melted, she hadn't used the Ouija board, and since moving to Grandaddy Opal's, she hadn't contacted any dead spirits whatsoever. I learned later that that had been the arrangement she and Grandaddy Opal had made. She would keep all her hocus-pocus outside of the house, and he would mind his own business and keep out of our way. Gigi didn't want him trying to turn me into a carpenter the way he had tried with Dane.

The day Gigi went looking for a job, I went exploring, looking through the drawers in the kitchen for the key to the basement door. That's where we had stored all of Dane's things. I had thought maybe I could set up a room down there, like Dane's old room, and light candle bottles and think about him, remember him. Already when I closed my eyes and tried to bring an image of him to my mind, I couldn't. I couldn't see him anymore, and I couldn't hear his voice. I thought being back in his room might help.

At last I found the key and I got so excited, I jammed it in the keyhole, flung open the door, and stepped so far out I missed the first step and fell down the others.

I landed with my head and shoulders on the last step and the rest of my body on the floor. A light came on and I heard Grandaddy Opal's voice shouting at me from above.

"What you doing down there?"

I sat up and my neck felt twisted funny. Blood ran down my left elbow.

"I fell," I said, staring at the blood.

"Well, be quiet about it."

"I didn't say anything." I struggled to stand. My left ankle felt like my neck, achy and twisted around.

"You were screaming all the way down," he said.

"No, I wasn't."

"Were too."

"Was not."

"You calling me a liar, child? You come on up here and let me have a look at you."

I climbed the stairs, going easy on my left ankle. Grandaddy Opal backed up into the main room and squinted down at me.

"She said you was a girl."

"I am a girl," I said.

"No, you ain't."

"Yes, I am."

"Are not."

"Are too."

Then he walked around me, slowly, like he was examining a sculpture in a museum.

"You're just like a pixie girl, ain't you? Why you wearing your hair all chopped up that way?" He picked up the bathrobe sash dangling from the loopholes around my waist and said, "No wonder you fell. What you dragging around in this old bathrobe for?"

"Gigi says I'm special," I said, using the same defense I used in school whenever I came under attack and couldn't think up anything better.

Grandaddy Opal moved his face right up to mine and said, "Don't you believe it, girlie. Don't you believe anything Gigi says." He straightened up. "Why, you're as common as a housefly." He wagged his head. "What's so special about you?"

"I was born from the body of a dead woman," I said, holding my chin up, daring him to say that wasn't special.

"Were not."

"Were too. My mama was hit and killed by an ambulance rushing to the scene of an accident. She was dead when they cut her open and pulled me out."

"Impossible," he said, shaking his shaggy head.

"No, it's not." I shifted my weight to my good ankle.

"Is too."

"Is not."

"Child, if your mama was dead when you were born, then you was never born. It's as plain as plain as that."

He said it, and I knew it was so.

Chapter 4

GRANDADDY OPAL'S WORDS played inside my head all the time, working their magic on me like one of Gigi's incantations. I even heard them in my sleep, in my dreams. *If your mama was dead when you were born, then you was never born.* I'd wake from my dreams and I'd be shivering and sweating at the same time. I'd look across the room at Gigi and watch her chest rising and falling, and I'd wait for my heart to stop racing. I'd try to push the memory of those words, dark and threatening in my dreams, out of my mind.

Sometimes I'd see Gigi twitch in her sleep or smack her lips or roll over mumbling something and I'd know she was dreaming. I'd rise up on my elbow and study her, the strips of light and dark that lay across her body transforming her into some other being. She'd be bald and her chin would be missing. I'd see only her nose and her mouth. Her forehead, spotlighted by the street-light that slipped between the window blinds, always looked white and huge. Behind it was where the dreams came from. That's what she said. I asked her about dreams one morning while she was putting on her makeup. I asked, "Are dreams real? Are they real life?"

She said, "Dreams are sending us messages. You understand, baby?"

"No," I said.

She turned to face me, one eye wearing false eyelashes and the other looking bald, blind. "Well, it's like this," she said. "Things go on during the day and it's just a lot of this and that happening. Then we go to sleep and our minds dig through all the stuff that's happened to us, even pulling out old stuff that happened long ago, and scrambles them into a dream."

She turned back to her mirror and, with her mouth wide open, applied the other row of lashes to her bald eyelid. Her ritual of applying makeup could take all morning. She used it to hide things, her age, her missing lashes, her unshapely brows and thin lips, whereas Aunt Casey wore makeup to enhance what was already there. This, I decided, was the main difference between the two of them, and back then I prefered Gigi's more flashy and exotic look. She finished applying her lashes and returned to the dreams.

"Now, if you think about your dreams and figure them out right, then you discover that they are giving you answers. They're giving you the truth about what's going on."

"But what about bad dreams?" I asked. "What do they mean?"

"Oh, bad dreams are warnings, or they're your fears. Or sometimes"—she looked at me through the mirror—"sometimes they're a sign of madness."

41

"Madness? Like a crazy person?"

Gigi nodded and lifted her eyebrow pencil to her brow. "Only cure I know is to hang dried orange peels above your bed and sleep with five cloves under your pillow."

"But how do you hang orange peels above your bed?"

Gigi gave me the instructions and I followed them exactly. I cut an orange into eight triangles, ate the insides, and threaded the triangles by poking a needle through their tips. Then I tied the orange peels to a coat hanger, screwed a hanging plant hook I'd found in one of the kitchen drawers into the ceiling above my bed, and hung the dangling orange peels on it. I slipped the cloves under my pillow and went to sleep. I dreamed a shadow was chasing me, trying to run me down. When I awoke, I found my shirt soaked in sweat. I remembered the shadow and I knew the shadow was mine. It was me, unborn, the truth about who I really was, an unborn child who had accidentally slipped out of place—a mistake. That's what I knew: I wasn't real, and this thought scared me so much I wanted to jump out of bed and run away somewhere. I wanted to run away from my own dark thoughts. I climbed out of bed and ran to the top of the basement steps. I stared down into the darkness and told myself, "Here's where I fell. Here's where I got *real* bruises and a *real* cut on my elbow. Grandaddy Opal had come to see. He heard me fall and had come to see if I was all right. Shadows don't bruise." Then I remembered what Grandaddy Opal had said about Mama. *If your mama was dead when you were born, then you was never born.* I changed it, right in my

42

head I changed it, so that Grandaddy Opal said to me, "Welcome to my home, young lady, glad to have you stay."

I remembered the fall that way from that night forward, and I stopped having the nightmares.

I wondered though, why, after such a nice welcome, Grandaddy Opal stayed hidden away in his bedroom. We had been living with him over three months and still I rarely saw him, almost never spoke to him, and I wanted to see him. Something about him reminded me of Dane. I thought I could remember Dane better, hold his memory closer, if I could see Grandaddy Opal again.

Gigi said I wasn't missing anything by not seeing him. "Anyway, he'd make you dull witted," she said, "the way he's always got to be looking something up in a book. Reading all the time locks up your brain so you're always thinking one way, and that way is never your own way. You understand me, sugar? It keeps you from perceiving and intuiting things. If you want to know something, you don't go look it up in a book. You put your question out there, out into the universe, and then you wait, and sure enough the information comes to you. Remember that, baby. You're better off without the attentions of that old man."

I always looked for him, though, hoping to see some hint of Dane in him, wondering what it would be like the next time we met.

One day the school bus pulled up in front of our house and I got off as usual, but this time Grandaddy was outside planting his vegetable garden. A large maple tree hid him from me and the other children on

43

the bus. When I climbed down the steps to the side-walk, some of the kids stuck their heads out the win-dows and shouted at me.

"Hey, girl, bet you're naked under that bathrobe." "Come on, what you got under there?" "Come on, sleepwalker, show us what you got."

Grandaddy Opal came jogging around the tree with a trowel in his hand, and he held it up and shook it at the kids hanging out the windows. The bus rolled away and the kids kept shouting, "Show us! Show us! Show us!"

Grandaddy Opal looked at me. "They doing that every day?"

I shrugged and looked away.

"Hey!" Grandaddy Opal tossed down his trowel. "You ever seen an old man walk on his hands before?"

I turned back to him and looked up at his craggy face. His hair was white and long, like angel hair, only it stood out from his head as if he spent most of his time standing on his hands.

"No," I said. "I've never seen an old man walking on his hands before."

"Well, just look-a here at this."

Grandaddy Opal put both hands on the grass, kicked up his legs until they were in the air bent at the knees, and he started walking on his hands. He walked like a mutant duck around the trunk of the maple tree and then waddled back to me, dropped down onto his feet, and stood up. His face had turned red and a large vein had popped out on his forehead.

"Now how about that?" He grinned, and I noticed he had Dane's mouth—small, thin lips that hinted at shyness. He had his eyes, too—the shape and the color were exactly the same—only Grandaddy Opal's eyes crinkled at the corners when he smiled and Dane's eyes looked flat, blank. I couldn't remember Dane ever really smiling.

"Hey, girl, you thought I couldn't walk on my hands, didn't you?" Grandaddy Opal said, pointing his finger at me. His grin got wider, exposing his brown teeth.

"No, I didn't."

"Yes, you did."

"No, I didn't, and anyways, I can do it, too."

"Cannot."

"Can too. I do it all the time."

"No, you don't."

"I do too. Watch."

I tossed my backpack on the ground, tightened the sash of my bathrobe, and kicked up onto my hands.

"See?"

"You ain't walking."

I walked around the maple tree and, then instead of coming forward on my feet to stand, I went into a back bend and stood up.

"Well, look at that! You're a springy little thing. You take gymnastics?"

I shook my head. "I don't want gymnastic lessons. I want to learn to dance."

"So learn already. What's stopping you?"

"I mean *really* learn, with real lessons and all."

"So do it!"

"Gigi says dancing is a waste of time."

"Maybe she don't know how good you are, huh?"

I hadn't thought of that, but I did that day, standing

45

beneath the sun in my grandfather's yard. I thought how dancing could be my special talent, the one Gigi always said she would discover, my prodigy talent. But how could she discover it if she never watched me dance, if she never let me have lessons?

"Gigi would be angry if I took lessons," I said, still going over the new thought in my mind.

"Is that so?" Grandaddy Opal said, leaning away from me and staring at me as if he'd never seen me before.

"Maybe."

"Maybe not. You really think you'd be any good?"

"Sure! If I had lessons I could dance even better than I can do gymnastics."

"Is that so?"

"Yes, that's so," I said.

"We got dance places here." Grandaddy Opal picked up his trowel and walked back to his garden. I followed him and stood behind him while he dug into the ground. The way he hung his head way down so his neck looked extra long reminded me of the times Dane would sit at his desk with his head bent low over a book, and I wanted to touch him, close my eyes and touch his sun-hot neck, and remember Dane.

"So how 'bout you taking lessons here?" Grandaddy Opal broke into my thoughts.

"Well, I don't know. Gigi wouldn't want me asking her about things like that."

"Hooey!" Grandaddy Opal tore open a packet of seeds and poured some into his dirt-dusted hand. He held them cupped at first, but then his hand started shaking so he had to fold his crooked fingers over them to keep them safe. "Tomorrow you and me's going to go looking for a dancing school. You like to dance, don't you?" He peered up at me through the strands of hair floating in front of his face.

"I love to dance!"

"All right then," he said, nodding. "All right, we'll find you a place."

I was so pleased about the idea of taking lessons, I danced around the edges of the garden while Grandaddy Opal huddled over his dirt and planted his seeds, one by one. I imagined myself a famous dancer, a prodigy at thirteen like Dane. I imagined Gigi so so proud of me, whisking me off to the seaside and feeding me tuna and tomato sandwiches, and watching me dance, dance, dance. And Dane would be there, too. I just knew he'd be there to see his great prodigy daughter perform. Maybe that's what he was waiting for. Maybe he'd come back when I was real, a prodigy.

I noticed Grandaddy Opal watching me, and I gave him my best arabesque, dipping my torso way down low where I could smell the dirt.

"Like a little spirit, you are," he said nodding. Then he went back to his seeds and I kept on dancing, just like a little spirit.

The next afternoon Grandaddy Opal told me that he'd done some calling around and he'd found a dancing school not more than a half mile from the house. "Cheap enough, too," he said, scooting along the sidewalk with me tagging after him trying to keep up. Grandaddy Opal walked or biked everywhere. He didn't own a car. He said he didn't trust them. "Best way to get anywheres is on your own steam," he told me. "Them automotives, trains, and planes, all of them can act up on you, even horses will give you a bad turn. No sir, I'll take walking or riding my Old Sam any day." So we walked, because I didn't own a bicycle.

The dance studio was in a church. It was in the fellowship hall, a big, square room. Folding chairs had been stacked on one side, and a long table with a large coffee pot in its center stood in the back. I liked to think about all the people dressed in their Sunday best, smiling even if they didn't know you, and serving coffee and juice and cookies. I went to church a couple of times, back when Gigi listened to what other people told her, and they told her I needed religion. We stopped going, though, because Gigi said there was more to it than the preacher was letting on. She said it was like the way the government doesn't admit that there are aliens from other planets roaming the earth. "That preacher's hiding too much up his puffy sleeves is what I think," she said. "He's got cards he ain't showing."

So we only went those two times, but I always remembered the nice preacher man and all the smiling faces and the smells of powder and perfume and coffee and polished wood.

The dance teacher's name was Susan. She told Grandaddy Opal and me to grab a chair, sit down, and watch her teach a class, then we could decide whether or not we wanted to sign up.

Just looking at all the girls lined up in their colorful tights and their pretty pink slippers—pink for femininity—made me want to jump up from my seat and join them, even if I didn't know any of the steps yet. Susan clapped her hands and all the girls got quiet. She demonstrated a plié and a grande plié, turning her feet out with her heels together and bending her knees. When she did the grande plié—a deep knee bend—her arm circled in front of her like a hair ribbon caught on a breeze.

Everything Susan did, I wanted to do. She kicked her leg up in the air and it went up past her head. She did leaps across the floor, springing high in the air with her legs split the way my Barbie doll's legs could split, and you could hardly hear her when she landed. The rest of the class sounded like a herd of elephants stampeding after her, but I knew I would be like her. I would be soft and light, and leap and spin just like her. I couldn't wait. I looked over at Grandaddy Opal to see if he liked it, too.

At the end of the class Susan called us over to explain her classes, when they met, and how much each one cost. Up close I could see she didn't wear makeup or shave under her arms, and she sat on the linoleum floor to talk to us with her legs spread out and her feet pointing and flexing, pointing and flexing.

Grandaddy Opal signed me up to go four afternoons a week: two ballet classes, one modern dance class, and one improvisation class.

Susan said that maybe I should just try one class at a time to see if I would like it, and Grandaddy Opal chuckled and said, "Oh, no need to worry about that, she'll like it all right," and he was right. Soon I would be a great prodigy, and Dane would come back and the two of us would go live by the sea.

I wanted to skip and leap my way down the sidewalk on our way home, but Grandaddy was dragging along, his hands dug deep into his pockets, his mind somewhere far away. I tried talking to him, telling him he wouldn't be sorry, telling him how good I was going to be, and then he just stopped dead and grabbed my hand. "Hey," he said. "There ain't no dance classes."

"Huh?" My mouth dropped open.

"You understand? As far as Gigi knows, there ain't no dance classes."

"Oh, okay," I said, nodding, not really sure if I understood, but wanting to keep the dance lessons.

"Okay then." He started walking again, faster, still holding my hand, dragging me with him along the sidewalk. "So we'll just say to ourselves there ain't no dance classes, then we won't make a slip and talk about them." He squeezed my hand tighter. "You go on over to that church every day, and I'll just think you're upstairs doing your homework. You're just doing your homework," he repeated, nodding to himself.

And that's how it was. My dance didn't exist. Every day I walked to the church. I did lunges and leaps and turns, and listened to Susan's voice correcting us over the sound of the music, and then I forgot it, because it wasn't real. While I was walking home, I knew a giant eraser followed behind me, erasing the dance class, rubbing it into dust and brushing it away, leaving behind an empty sidewalk, an empty past. Later, I started to run home every afternoon, afraid the eraser would catch up to me and erase me, too.

Chapter 5

GIGI LOOKED RELIEVED when I told her I wouldn't be able to help out down at the gift shop except on Fridays and Saturdays. She didn't even ask me why. Ever since we'd moved in with Grandaddy Opal, she had been like that, keeping to herself, sleeping late, working long hours at the shop. She even forgot my eleventh birthday.

I knew it was because she blamed me for Dane's melting. That's why she couldn't look at me or be bothered with caring for me anymore. She had figured out the truth about me, just as I had. She knew that I was a mistake, nothing special at all, not even real, and Dane had melted from the shame of it.

Back at our old house, when things were good and right and Dane still lived with us, Gigi used to get up in the mornings and fix me breakfast, and the two of us would tiptoe around and whisper so we wouldn't wake up Dane, and we always found something funny that we were just dying to laugh out loud at but couldn't because of Dane. Now, when there was no reason to be quiet, there was nothing funny, and Gigi didn't get up until after I'd gone off to school. If I wanted to see her at all, I had to go down to the gift shop.

She worked in a small room clouded with incense at the back of the shop. Mrs. Hewlett, who owned the shop, was a widow, and when she found out Gigi could contact the dead, she hired her right away. The first time Gigi contacted Harold, Mrs. Hewlett's dead husband, the woman cried for days afterward. "It was so real," I heard her tell someone in the gift shop once. "He was there, I saw him. And he said things, things that only he knew. And he was happy. That's what I needed to know, that he was happy. He'd had such a miserable death, you know."

Then when Mr. Hewlett, through Gigi, gave his wife a successful decorating tip for the shop and told her she would be a great success, Mrs. Hewlett set Gigi up with her own special place in the back. In no time, word got around about Gigi and she was in business, holding séances, contacting the dearly departed, and reading tarot cards and tea leaves, but she never used the Ouija board again.

At first I used to go to the shop and stand in the farthest, darkest corner, hidden from her clients, and just watch Gigi. She'd slip into one of her colorful robes, green for seeking knowledge of the beyond, white for ceremonies held on Mondays—moon days—sky blue for love, purple for Sundays. Then she'd dance around the table with circular motions—always circular to keep out evil—and she'd chant her incantations over the anxious client or clients who sat at the table with eyes closed, palms resting face up. She'd sit down then and light the candles, and slowly, with a circular, swaying motion in her torso, go into a trance, letting the spirits enter her body. Her voice would change. Sometimes she was Rasmus, her spirit guide, and other times she was the dearly departed. I would watch the way her skin turned yellow and her eyes rolled slowly forward before she opened them wide and focused on some unseen face.

Later, when Gigi had gotten used to my being there, I became her assistant. She didn't ask me to help her, I just offered to get her coffee one day and she let me. I was so pleased to get a chance to show her I could be useful that I began to rush about, helping her clean up in the evening, running out to the diner down the road to fetch her lunch, and bringing the footstool to her between clients so she could prop up her swollen feet.

I figured she must have been really pleased with me, because after a while she began to let me help her get ready for her ceremonies. I got to select the ingredients for the incense, choosing from rose, cedar, citron, aloe, cinnamon, sandal, camphor, amber, lily, benzoin, mace, saffron—she had so many jars and vials, and each combination of herbs, flowers, spices, and oils had a special meaning, was meant for special ceremonies. I learned them all.

I got to select the appropriate robe from Gigi's closet and help her slip into it, and I brought messages to Mrs. Hewlett at the front of the shop and led clients to their seats in the back.

One time Mrs. Hewlett said to me that maybe I

would become a medium like my grandmother, and I thought maybe I would. Maybe that would be my special gift. Maybe if I could do a good enough job, Gigi would see this and declare that I was a prodigy as a medium! Then she would forgive me for making Dane melt, and she would want me again, and Dane would come back, and everything would be right once more.

One day, after months of helping at the shop, I suggested to Gigi that I could do the dances for warding off evil while she concentrated on going beyond and reaching the dearly departed.

Gigi shook her head. "No, I'll do the dances."

"But I can do it," I told her. "I can help you. I can do the dances for you so your legs won't get tired. Watch, I can do it."

Then, before she could say anything, I started dancing around the table. I swept my arms up above my head and circled the table, two times, two representing social communion. My arms swung down, then up again. I leaned over the table, sweeping my torso in a low circle. In my mind I was a great ballerina. I pretended a crowd had gathered in the shop; all the kids from school who teased me about wearing Dane's bathrobe and who slammed dirt balls in my ears were watching. They stared wide eyed, stunned by my beauty and skill. I circled back in the other direction, my arms waving gracefully above my head. Someone was breaking through the crowd of kids. A man. A man was straining to see me over the heads of my audience. Dane! It was Dane! He had come to see my great performance.

"Miracle! I said to stop it!" Gigi caught one of my

arms in midflight and gripped it in her hands, pulling it down to my side.

"I do the dances," she said. "Anyway, you look ridiculous. From now on you had better just sit on that pillow over there and keep out of the way!" Gigi pointed to the large tiger-skin pillow that sat on the floor beneath a fan of swan feathers. "Go on."

I backed away. I didn't know what I had done, what evil spirit I had conjured up with my dance. I sat down on the pillow and closed my eyes and drifted far away, leaving behind the noise of Gigi's swishing robe, the clinking jars of incense, and Rasmus's murmurings. I went to a special place, a safe, new place. There were green fields and wildflowers there, and fairies and gnomes and distant castles poking through swirls of pink and white clouds. A blanket of butterflies flew overhead to greet me. Then they drifted down and settled about my shoulders and kept me warm and safe. No words, no dirt balls, no teacher, no child—nobody could reach me there, except Dane. I talked to Dane in my special new place.

I told him he was the first one to really see me dance, and he said my dance was beautiful. I told him about the dance recitals I could never be in because no one knew I took lessons. He said he understood, and the blanket of butterflies wrapped about me like a hug.

I told him about the giant eraser that swept down the street behind me every afternoon erasing my lessons, and how the other kids in class laughed at me because I couldn't remember the steps from one day to the next.

Dane was very sorry, and the gnomes and fairies nodded their heads; they were sorry, too.

"It's okay," I told them, shrugging off the blanket of butterflies. "I stand in the back of the room and I become invisible, just like in school. Most of the time I'm invisible."

Dane said he knew all about being invisible, and I asked him when he was coming back. When would I see him again?

"Soon," he said. "I'll be back soon." And I heard my own voice saying aloud, "Soon. Soon."

Chapter 6

NO ONE EVER talked about Dane. Not Gigi. Not Grandaddy Opal. When I tried to bring him up, to remember something about him, Gigi would go into a trance and Grandaddy Opal would just say, "Hooey!" But whenever Gigi and Grandaddy Opal got together, they fought, and they fought about Dane. I knew it even though they never mentioned his name. Sometimes Gigi and Grandaddy Opal would head for the bathroom at the same time and they'd see each other coming and race to the bathroom door, both trying to get there first. Grandaddy Opal always won because he was skinny and springy while Gigi was heavy and didn't like moving fast in the first place. It upset the karmic balance, she said. Grandaddy Opal would slam the door in her face and laugh a crazy man's laugh, and Gigi would stand in the hallway, chanting one of her spells at him.

They had other little wars, too. Gigi said Grandaddy Opal's orange La-Z-Boy had to go because it was giving off a bad aura left over from when Grandaddy Opal sat in it. She and I dragged it out to the sidewalk, and she put a big FREE sign on it, and it was gone by the next morning. Grandaddy Opal had a fit and a half and retaliated by dumping all of Gigi's fresh-bought macrobiotic food in the garbage. "I ain't having all that yin-yang food in my house," he said to her, the garbage truck rolling down the drive. "It gives off bad orals all over the durn place."

"It's aura," Gigi said. "A-U-R-A."

"Well, the plural of aura is orals," Grandaddy Opal shot back, embarrassed that Gigi caught him in a mistake.

That's the way it was. They tried to stay clear of each other, but when they couldn't, it was war, and even though no one said Dane's name, I knew somehow that's what the fighting was all about, because every time they fought, Dane was there. I could feel him. Gigi and Grandaddy Opal faced each other and argued, and Dane was the air between them, the hot angry air each of them breathed out of their mouths when they spoke. And when they stopped fighting and went their separate ways, the Dane vapors remained behind, and I'd stand in the midst of them and close my eyes, waiting for him to speak to me, to tell me that he was coming soon, but soon seemed to be getting farther and farther away. So were my chances of becoming any kind of prodigy, and every day I needed Dane even more than the day before. I needed to sit with him in his candlelit cave again and hear him read to me in his mellow voice, and feel safe and warm and content, because it seemed nothing felt safe anymore. Fear, like a shadow, hung about me, waiting. It wanted in. It wanted to take over my whole self. Every once in a while, I could feel the dark thing hovering, jabbing at me, looking for a way in, and my heart would begin to race and my palms to sweat. And then I'd think, it's that scary fear thing trying to get me. It hid everywhere, waiting for me to let go of Dane, let go of wanting to bring my daddy back, so that it could get inside me, and then Dane would never be able to come back to me. That's what I knew, and I searched everywhere for things to hold on to that would keep me safe, keep the fear away: simple, good things, like Grandaddy Opal's job. He delivered newspapers to all the houses in the neighborhood, and in the early mornings I would watch him from my bedroom window as he pedaled down the driveway on his bicycle, his newspaper bag draped over his shoulder and his long white hair flying like a wing from the back of his head.

I told Grandaddy Opal that delivering papers on a bicycle looked like the most fun thing to do—besides dancing, of course, but I didn't mention the dancing.

Grandaddy Opal said he would get me a bicycle and then I could join him on his route. It wouldn't be a new bicycle, though. He said it would be an old beat-up one picked up at a yard sale. He was good at fixing bicycles. "You fix it up, paint it, and then it's yours," he said. "You take care of it, grease it up good every now and then, give it a name, and you ride it everywhere. You and that bicycle become best friends. It's a real special relationship."

I couldn't wait to get one, to own something special, but Grandaddy Opal said it had to be the right one.

"Has to be cheap as dirt," he said, "and it's got to have personality. Don't worry, I'll know it when I see it. Meanwhile, I can teach you how to ride some on Old Sam."

We practiced in the late afternoons, after my dance lessons and before Gigi came home. Learning to ride was hard for me. Old Sam belonged to Grandaddy Opal, and he didn't want anybody but Grandaddy riding him. Even with the seat lowered all the way, I had to pedal with the tips of my toes and Grandaddy Opal had to hold on to the back of the seat to keep me steady. I couldn't wait to get my own bicycle.

We had been living with Grandaddy Opal well over a year—I was almost twelve—when he came into our bedroom one morning and shook me awake. I saw his empty newspaper pouch hanging around his neck like a feed bag.

He put his finger to his lips. "Shh." Then he told me to hurry up and get dressed. He left and I put on clothes from the day before, not worrying about making too much noise and waking Gigi. Since we'd been living with Grandaddy Opal, nothing woke Gigi before nine or ten in the morning.

I went out to the kitchen, but Grandaddy Opal wasn't there. I went into the great room, and that was empty, too. Then I saw him through the window, wheeling his bicycle out of the garage. I ran outside and called to him.

"Well, what took you so long?"

"I wasn't so long."

"Sure you were. Now, go on into that garage and see what you see."

I knew right then what I'd find, and I was right—my bicycle. I could see its dark form leaning against the washing machine, waiting for me. It didn't have the freshly painted shine of a just-fixed-up bicycle because Grandaddy Opal said I would have to do all the fixing and caring for it myself, that way it would become special, and really mine.

"That there is an old English racer," Grandaddy Opal said, coming into the garage and switching on a light. "And look-a here"—he pointed to a decal on the bar just below the seat. "See what that says? Nottingham, England. And see the picture of Robin Hood? Robin Hood was from Nottingham. You ever read about Robin Hood stealing from the rich to give to the poor?"

I nodded. I had written a book report on it for school and the teacher had read my paper to the class. Everyone said that I had made half of it up because they had seen the movie on TV and it didn't have all the stuff I had put in my report. Even when we all had to read the same book, I never understood it the way the rest of the class did. The teachers often called my responses to the book discussions "most disturbing."

I rubbed my finger over the decal. "Thank you, Grandaddy Opal," I said. "It's the most beautiful bicycle in the world."

"See on the front here it's got this plate nailed in that says made by the Raleigh Company. Yup, an English racer's what you got, girl. Bought it off an English lady, too, from Cambridge originally. So imagine that, this bicycle coming all the way from England when the woman first came over way back in 1964."

61

"Wow, it's old," I said.

"Paint's still good on her, too, just needs a bit of a touch-up and a polish. And I got some new tires so you can learn how to put them on, and I'll show you how to fix the brakes, they don't work at all, and it's got three speeds, but they ain't working neither. But look at her—so simple. She's sleek, that's what she is. Just like you, not an ounce of fat on her." Grandaddy Opal's face was all lit up with joy, as if it were his first bicycle instead of mine.

I held on to the handlebars with one hand and reached back and patted the cracked saddle with the other. "It's perfect," I said.

IT WAS HARD putting in the time to fix up my bicycle because of dancing and helping Gigi and going to school. One time, when it had been almost a week since I had last been able to work on it, Grandaddy Opal woke me at three in the morning and we worked on it then.

I told Grandaddy Opal that I hoped Gigi didn't catch us out in the garage working so early, even though I knew she never would, and Grandaddy Opal said it was all just a lot of fat hooey. "What does she think you live on, air? Why, you got to eat, don't you? Your clothes need cleaning, all them sweated-up leotards and tights, and you're growing, too. You need new clothes. How does she think it's all happening? Magic? She ain't doing it, that's for sure. And I shouldn't be doing it neither 'cause the day will come when she'll take a notion you're going to be the next great something or other and away you'll go from here!"

I looked away, feeling guilty for wishing I'd become a prodigy, but then I figured if Grandaddy Opal understood, if he knew the way I did that it was our only chance of getting Dane back, he'd wish it, too.

I turned back to Grandaddy Opal and watched him fussing with the wrenches. Then he bumped into his toolbox and all his tools crashed to the floor.

"Dang that Gigi!" he said, turning this way and that, looking at his mess.

I knew just thinking about Gigi could get Grandaddy Opal all worked up. It was as if he kept playing some old fight over in his head, trying to wring all the anger out of it one more time, maybe hoping this time would be the last.

"I guess we'll just go on pretending I don't even know you," he said, bending down to help me pick up his tools, his voice calming down again. "Even though you're living under my roof all the day long. We'll just pretend and say nothing to her. Long as we ain't saying nothing, we ain't bringing it to her mind, and she don't have to do nothing about it."

I finally finished fixing up my bicycle the night before my twelfth birthday. I wanted to ride it right away, but Grandaddy Opal said it was too dark and too late and I needed to get to bed before Gigi came home and had a fit.

I didn't want to go to bed. I didn't want to go to sleep and wake up to another birthday, to hear the story one more time of my birth, full of portents and omens. It was easier to be with Grandaddy Opal and forget. He always seemed to know when I was thinking too hard on things, when I was scared. He'd come up behind me and say, "Come on, girlie, let's go get us some watermelon," or "Let's go weed that garden." He always pulled me away from my thoughts.

Grandaddy Opal bought me a helmet for my birthday. He gave it to me in secret the next morning, waking me early and bringing me out to the dark garage. Then he switched on the overhead light and sang out "Happy birthday!" He set the shiny blue helmet on my head, the same color as my bicycle, and said, "Now then, you and Etain are ready to roll."

I had named my bicycle Etain after a woman in an old Irish tale I'd just read. She had been turned into a butterfly by another woman jealous of Etain's beauty, and then was blown by a magic storm out of the palace where she lived. After seven years she landed in a fairy palace where she fed on sweet honey flowers and loved a man named Angus. Then the evil woman discovered where Etain lived and she sent another storm that blew Etain out of the palace and into the drinking glass of a woman who swallowed her and later gave birth to her. When Etain grew up, she married the High King of Ireland.

Etain and I were perfect together. I was about to climb onto her when Grandaddy Opal spoke up, not looking at me but just to the side of me.

"Wonder if it would be easier without that old bathrobe you got on? Now that you're twelve and all."

I looked down at Dane's old black-and-yellow plaid robe. Gigi said they were the worst colors to wear together besides black and red, or just plain black—the evil colors. I think that's why Dane wore it in the first place, to spite Gigi. It had become faded and torn in the past two years and I had spilled all kinds of food on it—grape juice, spaghetti sauce, and chocolate— and it smelled of incense. Even when Grandaddy pulled it fresh out of the dryer, it still had the incense smells, but Grandaddy Opal never mentioned it, maybe never noticed.

In dance class, Susan said she needed to be able to see my body. She said she needed to make sure my knees were in line with my feet in a plié and that I didn't hitch my hips to one side in a *grande battement*. For Susan, I wore just the sash tied around my waist. She said I looked cool. The rest of the class said I still looked dumb.

I looked up at Grandaddy Opal. He was waiting, studying the shelf of paint cans off to his right.

"I'll just wear the sash, okay?"

Grandaddy Opal smiled at me and nodded. "Fine, fine," he said. "Now let's see you ride the old girl around in the driveway some."

Without thinking, I took off the robe. I was tying the sash around my waist when Grandaddy Opal grabbed my arm.

"What you got there?"

"What?"

He took my other hand in his and examined my arms and then my legs. I was in shorts and a sleeveless shirt. In dance I always wore long sleeves and tights. They hid the bruises.

"Where'd you get all these here?" He moved closer to me, his voice sounding strange, as if he could hardly get it out of his throat.

"You're all beat up. Look at you, you're all beat up!"

I looked down at myself, at the bruises on my legs. I looked back up at Grandaddy Opal, who had gone as white as his hair. Even his lips had turned pale. I felt my own self turn some kind of unnatural color, my stomach clutching and grabbing at my spleen.

I spoke. I whispered, with my head bent over the handlebars. "I didn't want to say because it's from you know where."

"What? I don't know where. I don't know nothing about this."

"Dance," I said. "My improvisation class. We do all this rolling around on the floor. We make up dances and express ourselves."

It was my turn to look away, at anything but Grandaddy Opal's face. He always wanted to see my eyes when he asked me a question, but I was afraid he'd know the truth. Susan had said something about it just that week. She didn't know about the bruises, but she saw the way I threw myself around in class, crashing to the floor, banging into the walls when the music was wild. I loved those classes, that wild feeling. I could spin and spin and fly all over the room, and nothing mattered, nothing existed but the sheer swirling ecstasy of the dance and the music. And when the dance was over, I had the bruises to remind me that for a little while, I felt real—I was a real, whole person.

I didn't know I was doing anything wrong until Susan called me out of the room. She placed her arm around my shoulder. She said she admired my expressive dances, but she worried that I might hurt myself.

"Keep away from the walls, will you?" she said. "And

don't do so many falls and recoveries. We don't want you breaking a leg, do we?"

"No, ma'am," I said, but I knew what she really meant. I knew she meant that I was "most disturbing."

I told her I would be more careful, and she let me go back to the class.

Grandaddy Opal's eyebrows rose clear up to the top of his forehead. "These here are from that dancing school? You can't be all that good if this is what you look like. You look at me, child. Do all them other little girls get banged up like this here?"

I didn't look up. I thought of the other girls in their colorful leotards and fancy leg warmers, the pretty hair ribbons, the dabs of makeup.

"Some are worse and some are better," I said. "I'm in between, I guess." I wouldn't look up. I couldn't. I was grabbing onto the handlebars, squeezing, squeezing them so hard I thought they might melt in my hands. My legs were trembling. I wanted to sit down, to breathe. There was no air in the garage.

"You look at *me!*" Grandaddy Opal's voice was sharp.

I lifted my head and caught his eyes, and my whole body started to shake. Grandaddy Opal's hair looked shocked as if an electric current were running through his head. His hands were trembling, and he brought them down on my handlebars, so close to mine I could feel their heat.

"You ain't going to have any more of these bruises, you hear? Whatever you got to do in that dance class to keep from getting them, you do it!"

I nodded my head and it kept on bobbing. My voice rattled in my throat. "Yes. Yes, we're through with that wild music anyway. We're doing something else now."

"You durn sure are or I don't know what!" he said. Then he blinked at me and I saw his eyes looking so wet, so full of water, and I had this vision of all that water pouring out from his eyes, gushing out like two giant waterfalls, rushing at me and knocking me over, carrying me far away.

Chapter 7

I DIDN'T KNOW if Grandaddy Opal had told Gigi about my bruises or not, but that night Gigi called me up from Grandaddy's basement where I had been sitting on Dane's bed, drifting in my fairyland, searching for Dane. I jumped up when she called because I didn't want her to come downstairs and see what I had done with all Dane's things.

I rushed up the stairs, and there stood Gigi with a stack of new clothes. She shoved them into my arms and told me I was emanating a green aura and I needed to stop wearing Dane's bathrobe. She waved her hands over my head, as if she could feel it, the halo of green light.

"Green is rarely good, sugar," she said. "It usually means you are putting yourself in someone else's place, allowing yourself to be taken over by him. Sometimes it even means deceit!" She grabbed both my shoulders. "Now you take off that old stinky robe of Dane's and put on these new spiritual clothes I bought you for your birthday. See if that doesn't help. Our years of mourning are at an end." She let go of me and lifted her arms above her head, her face turned to the ceiling. She closed her eyes and hummed. She opened her mouth, still humming, and then with a sudden snap of her lips she stopped. I waited several minutes for her to speak. Then, in a loud quivering voice, she said, "The winds of change are blowing." Her arms swayed above her. "The stars are realigning. You must be ready. Great things are about to happen to us all!" She opened her eyes and clasped my head in her hands. "You've been green way too long. You start wearing your spiritual clothes every day, you hear? You wear nothing but purple, and you meditate on the highest spiritual matters till you have a purple aura, like me. Purple means you possess spiritual and psychic powers. Now, go on and change and bring me that old robe when you're done." Then she turned and glided away.

I took a long time changing my clothes. I undid the sash of the robe and ran it back and forth through my hands, feeling the worn material slipping between my fingers. Then I set it on my cot and took off the robe. It was like peeling off all the layers of my skin. Anytime I removed it, I felt certain that I had become invisible, as if the robe gave my body its shape and substance. Without it I was nothing at all. I cut off a piece of the sash and stuffed it in my shorts pocket. I tied the rest of it around the robe, and after changing into my purple, carried it out to Gigi. I didn't watch to see where she put it. I went outside to Etain. We rode around and around in the driveway.

I wore my purple long-sleeved shirts and long pants

and waited through the sticky sweet heat of a Georgia summer for my bruises to disappear. And I watched while the winds of change blew through Grandaddy Opal's house, reshuffling all our lives.

They were little things at first. Gigi started getting up earlier to spend some time with me before she went off to the shop. Grandaddy Opal grew his tomatoes and cucumbers and shared them with Gigi without grumbling about her macrobiotic foods, and the two of them started talking in front of me as if they liked each other. I had visions of them someday getting remarried and all of us living happy lives together, just the way it was that summer, happy and slow and sweet.

I got to take over Grandaddy Opal's newspaper route and spend the money I earned on anything I wanted. I bought a beautiful illustrated set of Grimm's and Andersen's fairy tales and the rest of my money I spent on things for Etain, like a rearview mirror and new reflectors.

I still missed Dane, and I still looked for him, but for the first time in my life I felt a gentleness, a softness in the unfolding of each day. The dark fears that had hovered over me had faded to gray; the shadow kept its distance.

One evening, near the end of that summer, the three of us were sitting out on the porch eating tomato sandwiches and drinking root beer. The air felt cool and dry for a change, and we rocked in our chairs with our faces lifted to catch the breeze. I could feel contentment riding on that breeze, flowing from one to the other of us. It was the first time we had all sat together in the same place. It was the first time Gigi and

Grandaddy Opal were quiet, but all this didn't last; the winds of change kept shifting.

"Your van is blocking my view!" Grandaddy Opal said. "All them painted-on stars when I could be looking at the real thing." He sat up straighter and strained to see past the van. "I been studying on stars, and I want to see 'em, so you go on and move that durn van out of my view!"

Gigi kept rocking, holding her face up to the air. "You painted it, remember? I'll move the van when you've fixed the porch floor. It's so steep a person needs a seat belt on her chair just to keep from rocking herself into someone else's yard. And you're a carpenter. It's an embarrassment."

Grandaddy Opal jumped up from his chair and slammed inside. Gigi rocked even harder. "Good," she said, her rocking chair slipping toward the steps. "Finally some peace around here."

But Grandaddy Opal came back. He crept up behind Gigi with a piece of rope and before she could say "Dad-blast-it!" he had her tied to the chair.

"Hey, what do you think you're doing here?" Gigi said, twisting and fussing with the rope.

"Your seat belt," he said.

"This isn't a seat belt!"

"Is too." He jerked her chair back and forth, holding on to the back of it by the knobs. "See, you ain't flying into anyone's yard now, are you?"

"You untie me!"

"But you wanted a seat belt."

"And I'm saying this isn't a seat belt."

"What did you expect?" Grandaddy Opal chuckled,

glancing at me. "Custom designed, with stars and crystal balls and tarot cards painted all over it?"

"Yes," Gigi said, finally getting the rope turned around so she could untie herself. "And a seat belt with a horse's behind painted on yours!"

And that's when Grandaddy Opal's new career came to life. He painted seat belts. He made up a brochure and we stuck one in every newspaper I delivered. He put one up at the Piggly Wiggly, and Gigi set one in the windows of the gift shop and Ansel's Pub. I stuck one up in the gas station and even on the bulletin board at the church where I took my dancing lessons. Susan, my dance instructor, became Grandaddy Opal's first customer. He painted a copy of a Degas statue he had seen in one of the books in his bedroom. It was a ballet dancer standing with her feet slightly turned out, dressed in a full skirt and a long braid running down her back with a real ribbon tied on the end. Grandaddy Opal painted her side view. The girl had a dreaming, faraway look, so Grandaddy Opal painted above it the words "TO DANCE—TO DREAM." Susan was so pleased she showed everyone, even the kids in my dance classes.

I had hoped they would see it and want to be my partner when we had to perform combinations across the dance floor. I wanted them to see I had changed, I had a real job—I delivered newspapers—and I had people who took care of me, one who made me breakfast and worked at a gift shop and one who made me dinner and painted seat belts. I didn't dance wild anymore. I even bought a pretty pair of purple leg warmers and had started to grow my hair so I could wear ribbons like the other girls in the class. I felt proud and important, but the kids hadn't changed. They liked the seat belt, but not the seat belt painter's granddaughter.

After his success with Susan's car, other people started asking Grandaddy Opal to paint their seat belts. They would drop their cars off in our driveway and he'd sit all day inside the car drinking gallons of sweet tea and painting every seat belt special. Grandaddy Opal painted tennis racquets and golf clubs and footballs and baseballs. He painted flowers and ocean scenes and slogans. Especially popular were the team slogans and religious ones like JESUS SAVES and THE LORD IS MY COPILOT. Some were funny and some were lines from poems, and some were just people's names painted really fancy.

Whenever I could, I sat out in the driveway with him and watched him paint. It was the only chance I had anymore to spend time with him. Once when I went out there, he was painting a sailboat under the slogan I'D RATHER BE SAILING, and he said to me, "Ain't it a mystery?"

"What?" I asked.

"How we are. People, I mean. We always got to be wearing slogans and advertisements all over ourselves. Why, we're nothing more than walking billboards."

"But if people didn't want it, you wouldn't have your great seat belt painting business."

Grandaddy Opal nodded and wiped the sweat off his face with a rag he pulled out of his back pocket. "Sure enough, but it's interesting what people take pride in, ain't it? Painted gold dollar signs yesterday, little bitty ones on all four seat belts. Took me all day.

It's their identity—the fancy car, the bumper stickers, the big wheels—like they're afraid they'll forget who they are 'less they can flash it around all the do-dah day."

"Their identity?" I shifted my weight from one foot to the other. "Grandaddy Opal? If you were going to paint my seat belt, what would you paint?"

Grandaddy Opal paused with the paintbrush pointed at the sail of the boat. "Girl, if I was painting your seat belt, well, I wouldn't paint it atall. You ain't a billboard. No sir, I'd just plain leave it blank."

He said it, and I knew he was right.

Chapter 8

GRANDADDY OPAL hadn't been the only one affected by the winds of change. In the late fall, Gigi joined a group called The Other Realms, a group of mediums, clairvoyants, and channelers who got together monthly and planned conferences where people learned about the occult. For once Gigi had friends who called her up and came over to the house more than once, and who invited her to dinners and get-togethers. I asked Gigi about friends, since neither one of us ever had any before. She said the only people she ever got a chance to meet were her clients and they couldn't be her friends because it would destroy the mystery of her. "They have to believe I'm different," she said. "That I don't eat or sleep or go to the bathroom like normal people. They don't want to see me walking around town in a pair of jeans licking on an ice-cream cone. Someone like that wouldn't be able to contact the spirit world. Understand? They have to believe it's possible. They have to believe, or it won't work."

I understood. The mystery of me kept people away, also, or drew them to me, with their dirt balls and their eggs, anything they could throw.

Now that Gigi had joined The Other Realms, she became much more open and outspoken about what she did. She taught me about astral planes and mental planes and how a nebulous appearance of the astral body meant an imperfect development, and an ovoid appearance was a more perfect development. She said Grandaddy Opal and I had nebulous astral bodies and she had an ovoid one. She said there must be a special reason why I was nebulous. That it must have to do with the way I came into the world. I looked up the word nebulous in the dictionary. It means hazy, indistinct. I closed my eyes after looking up the word and I knew what Gigi said was so. I felt nebulous.

Grandaddy Opal knew about The Other Realms group, and he reminded Gigi of their agreement. Gigi said she wasn't doing anything in his house. The place wasn't filled with incense or candles, and if he'd ignore her doings she'd ignore his. This she said looking pointedly at me. Grandaddy Opal muttered and cussed and Gigi said, "Why, you're just afraid. You're just like everybody else. You know what occult means? It means it's beyond the range of ordinary knowledge. So now, why are people so afraid of knowing more?"

" 'Cause some of that stuff we oughtn't to be knowing, that's why," Grandaddy Opal said. "It's dangerous getting into that business, and you had better leave Miracle out of it."

"Don't you tell me!" Gigi said.

Whenever I heard those words, I knew in no time

we'd be in the van heading back to Alabama and Uncle Toole and Aunt Casey. Every time Grandaddy Opal made any suggestion to Gigi about raising me, Gigi would tell him a thing or two, go to the bedroom, pull our suitcases down from the closet, and order me to start packing.

I would try to take my time packing my bag, giving Gigi a chance to change her mind, but she would always get irritated with me and shove me aside so she could pack the bag herself. I would stand in the doorway, knowing I was supposed to stay with her and watch, but when I felt she wasn't noticing, I'd twist my head and look down the hallway, my heart beating against my chest in quick trembly rhythms, hoping Grandaddy Opal would be there and he'd say some magic words that would make Gigi want to stay. But Grandaddy Opal had a stubborn streak just as wide as Gigi's, and as soon as she'd make her decision to leave, he would take off on Old Sam and the last I'd see of him would be his back.

We wouldn't be on the road more than an hour before Gigi would think up some reason why we needed to turn around again, but I always feared the day would come when she would run out of good excuses and off we'd ride, getting farther and farther away from my sweet Grandaddy Opal.

One time, she pulled off to the side of the road and turned to me and said, "That's Dane's house he's living in. Dane bought it. Your grandaddy doesn't have any more right to it than we do. Why, we have more of a right to it really. I'm the one who raised Dane. If it weren't for me, he never would have had enough money to move that old man out of his apartment and buy him a house. Come on, we're going back." Then she turned the car around and back we went to Grandaddy Opal's.

That's how I learned about Dane buying Grandaddy his house, and I figured if this house really did belong to Dane, then Dane would be coming here when he returned, not back to our old, rented house. He'd be coming here, back to us, I just knew it. Then a few days after Gigi had told me about the house, Aunt Casey came for a visit, which she did about every two months or so, and she proved to me that I was right. I came right out and asked her about Dane owning the house, and she nodded and said that he and Grandaddy Opal had been real close.

"Yeah, I could tell Dane loved his daddy," she said, sticking her wad of chewing gum under the seat of her rocking chair and lighting up a cigarette.

"Said he got his artistic talents from him, not from Gigi, like Gigi's always implying. Of course, what I know about prodigies is that they don't really get it from anyone except God. It's not inherited, it's a freak thing. But Dane liked to say he got it from your grandaddy." Aunt Casey laughed and smoke came out of her mouth. "It riles Gigi good, I can tell you." She nodded. "Yes indeed, Dane loved his daddy." She rocked awhile then, out on Grandaddy's slipped-down porch, and I rocked with her, chewing on the piece of gum she had given me and thinking over what she had said. If being a prodigy came from God, how was I supposed to become one? I didn't have much time left. I would be thirteen soon, the age Dane had been when his first book came out. What would happen to me if I never became a great dancer, or I never developed any supernatural powers like Gigi? Then Dane never would come back, even if the house did belong to him.

A new thought struck me. Maybe I'd disappear. Maybe on my thirteenth birthday I'd just melt. I sat chewing on my gum thinking about this, and that's when Aunt Casey said, "Remember way back when Dane disappeared?"

I stopped rocking. No one had mentioned Dane and his melting since it had happened and just hearing her bring it up, as if she were reading my mind, gave me a strange, spinning feeling in my head, and I had to suck in a big breath of air and let it out again before I could speak.

"You mean when he melted?" I said.

"Yeah, okay. Well, I thought for sure what had happened was he had run off here. I thought he had run off to be with his daddy."

"But he didn't, right?" I said, looking over my shoulder, hoping against hope that he would be standing behind me smiling, that he and Aunt Casey had cooked up this great surprise for me. But the porch was empty. I turned back around. "He's not here. We're here. It's just me and Gigi, come to live with Grandaddy Opal."

"Yeah, I wondered awhile about that. Why would Gigi come live with her ex-husband after all the tugging and fighting they did over Dane, and after she walked out on him? And you know what I figured?"

"What?"

Aunt Casey took a long, slow drag off her cigarette and blew the smoke out through her nose. We both watched it swirl up and up and dissolve slowly in the air, like an astral body.

"I think she's waiting for him." Aunt Casey took another drag and nodded. "I bet she thinks Dane's coming back, and when he does, he's coming here."

She said it, and I knew it was so.

Chapter 9

WAITING. That's what we had been doing. We had all been waiting for Dane. That's why no one dared speak his name. It held too much hope, too much expectancy. It's why Gigi hid out in the back of the gift shop until that summer when she met her Other Realms friends. Even Grandaddy Opal had sat in his room all day, listening for Dane's footsteps on his front porch. Even he had been waiting. But then, after Grandaddy Opal found all those bruises on me, it all changed. My bruises were a signal of some sort. I didn't understand it, but I knew that all the changes, the way they seemed to have stopped waiting, had to do with the bruises. I was pushing them away somehow, from Dane, and from me, but I couldn't help the bruises anymore.

I spent most of my days on my own after Grandaddy Opal went into the seat belt painting business and Gigi joined The Other Realms. In the afternoons I would go down to the basement and sit on Dane's bed surrounded by the candle bottles I had dug up out of one of the boxes, and I'd read stories or go to my fairyland and talk to Dane. Every time after I visited with him and asked him my questions—Why did you melt? Where are you? When are you coming back?—I needed to dance my wild dances. I'd go upstairs and push all the furniture against the walls to make room for them. I'd put on music, first Grandaddy Opal's old Patsy Cline albums so I could start out slowly, moving just my hands, making shapes. Sometimes, I practiced melting to the slow music, testing it out, in case it would be my turn someday. It didn't feel as scary as I thought it would be. I moved slowly, easily, feeling my body go limp, part by part, starting with the head and sliding down to the legs, down to the floor, where I'd lie still, a melted puddle, my eyes closed, feeling the beat of the music against my body. I imagined myself melting into the floor and then deeper, into the earth, deeper still, below the earth, beyond the earth. Then where? Where did Dane go then? There's where I always got stuck. I could never imagine what lay beyond the earth. All I knew was Gigi's world of spirits and spirit guides, and they were all people who had died and were caught in the ether world. But Dane wasn't dead, so he wasn't with the spirits. What else lay beyond the earth?

When my thoughts got too disturbing—most disturbing—I would jump up from the floor and put on one of Dane's Bob Dylan tapes, or some of his exciting-sounding classical tapes, and dance wild. I danced, shook, and rattled the thoughts clear out of me. I danced until I felt the ecstasy, until I felt the bruises.

When I could hear my heart pounding in my ears,

when every muscle and bone ached beyond endurance, I stopped. I turned off the music and went to my room and flopped down on the cot, breathing hard, listening to my heart beating in my ears.

Sometimes I turned on the old black-and-white TV set. It was still broken. I turned it on and off, on and off. When I turned it on, the screen flashed with light, but when I turned it off, the light would shrink, getting smaller and smaller until it was just a pinpoint in the center of the screen. I watched it, fascinated, getting up closer to see if I could see inside the light, maybe see Dane, before it went out.

Grandaddy Opal caught me staring into the tiny light one time and he said, "What you doing there? I been hearing you turning that durn thing on and off near a hundred times at least. You think that's going to fix it?"

I jumped away from the set. "I like seeing the light go out."

"What light you talking about?" Grandaddy Opal came into the room wiping his paint-splattered hands on a rag and stuffing it back in his pocket.

"Watch." I turned the set on for a few seconds, then turned it off. I did it three times and then did it two more times real fast so it would count as five times because Gigi said bad things happen in threes. Numbers and other superstitions were becoming more important to me then. Gigi's rules about numbers and colors made me feel safe, less afraid of that dark emptiness I had discovered that lay beyond the earth. Sometimes, when no one was around, I got the feeling that maybe I was slipping into that empty, nowhere place. I could feel it happening and I'd look around, searching for something to hold on to, but there was never anything there anymore.

Grandaddy Opal got up real close to the TV the way I had been. He squinted at the screen and shook his head. "Well, how do you like that? I'd forgotten how the black-and-whites always did that. I've got a color TV set in my room."

I nodded. "And it works."

Grandaddy Opal pointed at the set. "Do that again. Go on, let me see it go on and off again."

I did it seven times. Odd numbers were good, even threes sometimes, but I wasn't sure when threes were good and when they were evil. Gigi said there was divinity in odd numbers. I liked the numbers five and seven—they were safe, no evil side to them.

"You know what that puts me in mind of?" Grandaddy Opal asked, backing away from the TV.

"No, what?"

He grinned at me and his eyes flashed as if tiny bits of light were dancing in them. Even his angel hair, still charged with the static from the TV, appeared to be dancing.

"Come on and I'll show you," he said, prancing out of the room and down the hall.

I followed close behind him, eager to see what he had. He stopped outside his own door and I held my breath. I'd been living with Grandaddy Opal over two years and I'd never seen inside his room. He opened his door only halfway and the two of us slipped sideways through the opening. When I was clear of the door, I let out my breath and looked around.

Grandaddy Opal's whole life was crammed into the very cracks and crevices of his tiny space. He had a cot like ours and an old stuffed chair with half the stuffing popping out of the armrests. The chair faced the TV set, and the set sat on a shelf that Grandaddy Opal must have made. It held everything—his books, an ancient bicycle wheel, lots of radio equipment that he said let him tune into programs and communications from all over the world, a stack of yellowed newspapers, some of his painting equipment, carpentry stuff, and bicycle fix-it tools. Empty Coke cans lined one wall, pyramid style, all the way to the ceiling, and he was starting another one to the side of his TV-watching chair. I was so overwhelmed by all his wires and tools and books I'd forgotten why we were there.

"Now let me see," Grandaddy Opal said, running his fingers along the rows of books. He had art books and bicycle books and science books and how-to-build-it books and the whole set of *Encyclopaedia Britannica*. On the bottom shelf were books on writing.

"Were you a writer, too?" I asked, stooping down and fingering one of the books.

Grandaddy Opal slapped my hand away. "Keep off of those."

I jumped back up. "But were you?"

"Nah, I was just interested in how it all works. I'm a self-educated man, you know." He pulled a book off the shelf and opened it up. "Here's what I wanted to show you. This here chapter is about black holes." He looked up at me. "Ever hear of them?"

"No."

"Hah! Didn't think so. You know what a star is, don't you?"

"Sure," I said. "Those lights in the sky."

"They're made of gas, you know that?"

I nodded. "I learned it in school. It's hydrogen gas, mostly."

"Did you know stars can run out of gas?"

"Like a car, you mean?"

"Kinda," he said. "The star just gets so hot and gives off all that gas until it uses it all up and then guess what?"

I shrugged and tried to peer over his shoulder at the book. He pulled it away. "I'm telling this," he said. He put his finger on a spot in the book and continued.

"See, what happens is the star, once it loses all its fuel, starts to cool off and shrink, like the light on your TV set, and then once it shrinks enough, gravity pulls on the star." He looked up from the book. "Now here's where it gets interesting. The gravity is pulling on the star so much that the light, instead of being sent out in the universe so's we can see it, gets turned inward, like pulling on a sock and turning it inside out. See, and if you pull that sock inside out and all the light was on the outside of the sock and now it's on the inside, well, then you have a black hole, because without the light you can't see it, and the light can't escape back out the hole. It's invisible. Just like staring into a TV set when it's off. Now imagine all the invisible holes in the sky up there. And you know what scientists think about black holes?"

I shook my head.

"They think that if we could go inside one and survive all that gravity pulling on us we could travel back in time! Now how about that?"

"Back in time? Where does it say that?" I said, grabbing his arm and pulling the book toward me, trying to see the words. "Say it again. Say about going back in time."

Grandaddy pointed to the words. "See, space and time fold in on themselves in a black hole, so if you passed through it you'd go back in time. They say no one's ever done it for real. All that gravity pulling on us every which way would tear our bodies apart before we could get too far."

"But—what about something melted?"

"Melted! Like another planet? Like ice cream?" Grandaddy Opal shook his head. "I don't know nothing about melted."

I studied Grandaddy Opal's face. Was he trying to tell me something? Trying to pass me a secret message? Was he saying, without really saying, that Dane had traveled back in time? Was he saying it in a way Gigi would never find out he told? Was that what we were waiting for? Had Dane melted into a black hole?

Grandaddy Opal scrunched his nose up at me. Then he looked down at my hand still grabbing onto his arm. "You're cutting into me with them nails of yours, girlie. Let go." He yanked himself away, and the book fell to the floor.

I stared down at the cover of the book. "Black holes," I said.

"Yup," Grandaddy Opal stooped down for the book. "And they talk about wormholes up there in those black holes and they say if you could pass through a worm-hole then you could come out in some different universe altogether. Now that's fascinating, ain't it?"

"Wormholes?" I said, still staring at the book, trying to think, trying to put it all together.

Grandaddy started talking about going back to the age of the dinosaurs, pretending he didn't just pass me the secret message, and I just knew I needed to get away. My mind was racing. I needed to be by myself and think, slowly, carefully. Think about melting and black holes.

"Excuse me, Grandaddy, I've got to go to the bath-room," I said, backing out of his room and leaving him in midsentence with his mouth open.

I ran to the bathroom and closed the door and locked it. I climbed inside the bathtub, pulled the shower curtain, and sat down to think.

What if Dane melted so he could go back in time? It's possible, isn't it? If he did, then he was probably going back to the time just before Mama got hit by the ambulance. He's probably making sure she doesn't go to town to see the doctor that day. He's keeping her at home, reading poetry to her or that Kafka story about the man who turned into a cockroach that he liked so much. Yes! He's reading to her, and she's only half listening while she rocks in her chair, resting her hands on her belly, on me, and thinking about how it's going to be—Dane, and her, and me, the new baby, living in a cottage by the sea. She's thinking about me growing up, playing in the sand and sunshine, running with the other girls and boys, going to school and having friends and teachers who understand me. And we're happy.

Dane is writing new books, and Mama is singing and fixing me tuna and tomato sandwiches and buying me clothes—red, yellow, green, and orange clothes, no purple. We wouldn't need purple. Yes, Dane melted. He did it for me! And just like Aunt Casey said, like Dane himself had whispered to me, he's coming back, and he's coming with Mama. He's coming here! That's why we've all been waiting, why nobody can breathe his name. He's on an important mission and we don't dare disturb the atmosphere. Dane and Mama, they are the true winds of change!

Chapter 10

I DANCED NEW DANCES. I didn't push back the furniture in the great room anymore, I danced all over it. The twin towers of *National Geographics* that stood alone ever since Gigi threw out the old La-Z-Boy toppled over and I danced on them, too. I created special dances for Dane and Mama, beautiful dance stories about our new life, the way it was going to be. Every chance I got I was dancing, living the dream in my mind, living it so much it seemed more real to me than the world around me, more wonderful.

Gigi almost caught me dance-dreaming one day when she came into the house with her new friend, Mr. Eugene Wadell. I had just leaped from one piece of the sectional sofa to the other when I saw Mr. Eugene Wadell opening our front door and bowing to let Gigi enter. I jumped off the couch and sat down in the pile of *National Geographics*, picking one up and opening it as if I had been sitting there reading all along.

Gigi entered the room with her smiling eyes on

Mr. Eugene Wadell, so it took her a few seconds to even notice me.

"Mercy, what a mess!" she said, when she did notice. "Miracle, what are you doing?"

I held up my magazine. "I'm going through all these *National Geographics*."

"What a ridiculous thing to do." She glanced at Mr. Eugene Wadell for confirmation and then returned to me.

"Your aura's changed from green to yellow-orange. Did you know that?" she said, and I knew she was showing off.

"It means you're thinking too much about yourself. That's typical for a soon-to-be teenager, I suppose." She turned to Mr. Eugene Wadell. "She'll be thirteen in just two weeks, and she's growing like a weed."

He nodded and opened his mouth as if he were saying "Ah," but no sound came out.

Gigi came back to me. "You just keep wearing your purple, now, you hear?" Then she stepped over the magazines and went off to our bedroom, leaving me alone with the funny-looking Mr. Eugene Wadell.

He was standing in front of me, nodding and looking like a bowling pin about to tip over. His hair grew out more on one side than the other and it made him look lopsided, as if he'd have a limp when he walked.

"That's right," he said. "You wear your purple. It will help bring you in touch with the spirit world." He stopped Dane's Mozart tape and nodded some more in the uncomfortable silence he created.

I tried not to stare at his big belly, the way it jiggled when he moved even the slightest bit. I hung my head over the magazine in my lap and pretended to read about the rainforest.

A few minutes later Gigi returned with a purple boa draped around her shoulders and a different pair of shoes, ones with higher heels.

She pulled on Mr. Eugene Wadell's sleeve and the two of them left, leaving me still sitting in the pile of magazines, listening to the *click-click* of her high heels and the *pat-pat* of Mr. Eugene Wadell's Hush Puppies going down the porch.

I wondered about her and that Mr. Eugene Wadell. She had been going out with him a lot. She met him at one of her Other Realms conferences and at first she said she didn't like him because he kept following her around and staring at her. Then it turned out both of them had the same spirit guide, Rasmus. Gigi said she didn't know that it was possible to have the same guide, but Mr. Eugene Wadell assured her it was.

Aunt Casey told me it wasn't like Gigi to fall for such a line and that he must have some good qualities we didn't know about.

" 'Course personally I think he's an A-number-one slimeball," she said. "He never smiles, he leers, did you notice? He leers at you like he's the Big Bad Wolf come to eat Granny and her Little Red Riding Hood."

I tried to talk to Grandaddy Opal about Gigi's new friend, but he was too busy with his own friend, Miss Emmaline Wilson, to pay it much mind. Miss Emmaline was a gospel singer with a voice so rich and strong she could topple the *National Geographic* towers without moving anything but her mouth. Even her speaking voice was loud. It was better if you could listen to her from another room instead of being right there with her.

She liked to pull one of Grandaddy Opal's rockers off the porch, set it down by the car he was working on, and yell at him while he painted. I could hear her clear inside the house with all the windows shut. Grandaddy Opal didn't seem to mind her talking voice at all. He said he was getting hard of hearing anyway.

Both Miss Emmaline Wilson and Mr. Eugene Wadell had been invited to my thirteenth birthday dinner, and for once I was looking forward to my birthday, even with the dreaded guests, because I knew Dane and Mama were coming home. I knew it the moment I woke up. I could feel it in the air.

Everything was still that day, no movement in the trees, no birds flying or singing, no squirrels scrambling onto the branches. Gigi always said that when animals stay in their nests and burrows and gathered nuts and berries are left on the ground, when even the wind doesn't stir, it is the foretelling of a cataclysmic event, and on that day, the beginning of my fourteenth year of life, everything, every creature, was waiting with held breaths for the great arrival of Mama and Dane.

Gigi planned my birthday dinner for four in the afternoon, so I spent the morning cutting my own hair, trying to get it to look like Dane's again. I didn't use a mirror, I just felt along with my hands, holding up the wisps and snipping them until it felt just right. Then I climbed onto Etain and rode her around the neighborhood, spotting abandoned nuts, and daring a single leaf to twitch, flutter, or fall. I felt a zinging tingling in my spine, a pricking of my thumbs, and I searched the darkened sky for signs of their coming. I just knew Dane and Mama were coming that day.

I had finished looking for signs and riding around the neighborhood by ten o'clock and still had so much of the day left before the party. I tried to settle down at the table in the great room with my notebook and a small stack of newspapers and magazines. These were special papers. Each one of them had a miracle story in them. That was my new hobby. I collected miracle stories. I cut them out of the newspaper or magazines and glued them in my special notebook.

Aunt Casey said I was collecting them as a way of connecting with my past, with the story of my birth. That was Aunt Casey's new hobby, analyzing people. She took psychology courses at the university to give her something to do at night while Uncle Toole was busy doing nobody-knew-what, and, as Gigi said, suddenly she was an expert on everything.

Gigi didn't like it one bit. Especially after Aunt Casey told her the reason Gigi wore robes all the time was to hide all the disappointments in her life. It made sense to me until Gigi took me to one of her Other Realms conferences and just about everyone there was walking around in long robes.

I had planned to mention this to Aunt Casey and see what she had to say about it, but she didn't come around so much anymore.

She came for my birthday, though. So did Uncle Toole, right in the middle of my cutting out the article with the headline MIRACLE RESCUE SAVES MOTHER, CHILDREN. I heard them outside talking, or rather I heard Miss Emmaline Wilson saying how she was pleased to meet them and how she met Grandaddy Opal through his seat belt painting business and asking if Uncle Toole was any relation to the Hillard Dawseys of Tuggee Creek.

I looked out the window and saw them coming toward the house, so I shoved the article in my notebook and stood up.

"Miracle! What on earth happened to your hair?" Aunt Casey asked as soon as she saw me. I opened my mouth to speak, but she jumped in before I could say anything.

"Even I don't think I can fix that shag-rag mess unless we just shave it all off. If you had thick curly hair it wouldn't be so noticeable, but you've got that straight wispy stuff. Why didn't you wait for me?"

Uncle Toole closed the door behind him and joined us, looking back over his shoulder through the window. Then he turned around and said, "That's a black woman he's got out there with him."

Aunt Casey shifted her weight so one hip bone was poking way out of her spandex, slapped her hand on the hip, and said, "No kidding. What was your first clue?"

Toole swatted her behind. "Don't you be acting so smarty. You just think you know it all. Running around like a bitty coed, acting no older than Miracle."

"I'm running around! You say *I'm* running around? Well let me tell you, Toole Dawsey—"

Aunt Casey never got to finish what she was going to tell him because Grandaddy Opal and Miss Emmaline Wilson came in, and Grandaddy said he'd just heard a tornado warning over the radio. I looked out the window. A green-gray aura hovered over the neighborhood. Dane and Mama were on their way!

Grandaddy moved to the windows and started opening them. "Miracle," he said, "go open the windows in your bedroom."

Before I could do as he said, Gigi and Mr. Eugene Wadell burst into the house. "A tornado's coming, we need to get to the basement," Gigi said, moving toward the basement door. She opened it and paused, waiting for us all to move. "Come on, don't waste time with windows, let's go!"

Then we all moved at once, with Uncle Toole trying to push through the bunch of us so he could get down the steps first. And first he was, riding down on his bottom calling out *Whoa! Whoa!* again, with his cowboy boots digging into nothing, the same way he did the night Dane disappeared. And that wasn't the only coincidence.

Grandaddy Opal's basement was one large room, but he had said I could fix up one section of it any way I wanted. "A person's gotta have a place they can call their own," he said when I asked if it would be all right. Gigi didn't know about it. No one did. Not even Grandaddy Opal, really. He'd never seen what I had done. He wouldn't recognize it anyway. He had never seen Dane's room, his cave. That's what was down there, Dane's room, just the way he left it. It had been easy to do. We had to store his furniture and boxes of stuff down there anyway. I just pulled some of it out and set it up. I pushed the writing desk up under the window and set the picture of Mama at the gate on it. I tucked his bed in the corner against the wall so Dane wouldn't fall out when he rolled on his right side. He always fell out when he rolled to his right. I changed the sheets every week and set the piece of bathrobe sash I had saved on his pillow. I arranged the bookshelves so they formed the walls of my room and lined them with all his books, Joyce and Sartre and Kafka—all his favorites. On top of the shelves and on his desk, all around his room, I had placed the candle bottles, and lately I had been going down into the cellar, lighting some of the candles, and doing my new dances there. I'd dance with the shadow on the wall. Dane's shadow. And I would thank him for melting, for trying to save me.

So there it was, just as it had been the night Dane disappeared, only the candle bottles weren't lit, and I couldn't help but think these coincidences were proof that Dane was coming home! He and Mama were going to show up any minute. I could see it, Dane and Mama still melted, still atomic particles dissolved in the air, swirling together into the tornado. And I could see the tornado touching down and releasing them, and they would be whole again. And at that same moment, the very moment their feet touched the earth, I too would become whole, not nebulous or blank or empty, but real. It was the perfect plan. I wanted to light the candle bottles and draw myself up on Dane's bed and wait. I wanted to close my eyes and feel them coming, feel the atmosphere around me changing, but everyone was there, and everyone had something to say about my room.

Gigi just about passed out when she saw it, falling against one of the walls and holding the back of her hand to her head and exclaiming, "Oh my! Oh my!"

Aunt Casey declared it was a shrine to Dane and I was worshiping a man I'd never really known. She said I needed a good talking to and if Gigi didn't do it soon, she would.

Uncle Toole said it was creepy, and Mr. Eugene Wadell stood in the midst of the candle bottles and claimed he was receiving mysterious vibrations from them. Aunt Casey told him to hush up and stay out of it, and Grandaddy Opal wanted to know what the hey was going on. Then Mr. Wadell bent down to pick up one of the candle bottles and I let out a scream because I didn't want that man to touch anything of Dane's. Miss Emmaline sang out in the same key as my scream and held it until we all shut our mouths. Then she started singing a song called "Amazing Grace." Her voice could take one word in the song and run it through about fifteen different notes before picking up the next word and chasing it up and down the scale as well. The whole room felt charged with her high-voltage voice. It made my hair stand on end and the candle bottles rock. All of us just froze in our places and listened to her, and no one could take their eyes off her, least of all me.

When she reached the end of the verse, she started all over again with the same words: *Amazing Grace, how sweet the sound, that saved a wretch like me. I once was lost but now I'm found, was blind but now I see.*

I listened every time, to every word, and by about the fifth time I was singing along with her inside my head, as if that's where the words had come from in the first place. It was just me and this voice—this rich, beautiful voice that sang my words, words I knew had

99

somehow come from within me. Miss Emmaline just happened to hear them and was translating them.

About the seventh time through, I felt so moved, I rose up off the bed, drifted past the candle bottles and the bookshelves to the open space, and I danced. And for the first time I understood what Susan had always told me. She said I needed to feel the music, feel the pulse inside me, speak it with my body. That night I did it. That night I remembered the lessons, each class, each combination, they were all there, all the classes that I had erased came back to me. It was all there in my head, in my body. It was a miracle! And I knew when I stopped, when Miss Emmaline Wilson stopped, that we had done something special together.

I waited for Gigi to say something. I waited for her to jump up and say, "See my prodigy! We have another prodigy in the family! Dane is surely coming back, and when he does, we will go to the sea and rent a little place, and we will fix her tuna and tomato sandwiches, and let her dance, dance, dance!"

Gigi opened and closed her mouth several times before anything came out and finally she said, "When—where—how did she learn that? What's been going on behind my back, Opal? Well?"

I didn't know where to look. Grandaddy Opal was hanging his head and picking at the dry paint on his hands, and I could tell Aunt Casey knew all about the lessons because she had gotten real interested in Mama's picture all of a sudden. Uncle Toole was squinting up his eyes in that everybody-knows-something-but-me way he had, even though I was sure he knew, too, but had probably forgotten.

"Opal, how could you?"

Grandaddy Opal lifted his head and spoke, his voice angry and his hair dancing wildly on his head. "Gigi, you can't do this. She has a right to follow her own..."

"No! No, it isn't her own, and you know it. You did this to spite me. To get back at me."

"You listen here." Grandaddy Opal pointed his shaky finger at Gigi. "That child has a right to..."

"I decide what rights she has. *I* decide!" Gigi's arms were flapping up and down as if she were drowning in a pool.

"You? You hardly know she's here."

"You knew I didn't want her dancing. You knew it! How could you do this to me?" Gigi turned to Aunt Casey. "Do you believe this? Behind our backs?"

Aunt Casey looked up from Mama's picture and glanced at Opal and then Uncle Toole and finally settled on Gigi. "Just leave it, Gigi," she said. "It's done, leave it."

Then out of the blue, Uncle Toole jumped in, pointing at Miss Emmaline and saying, "Are we all just going to pretend she ain't black? Old man Opal's going around with a black woman at least twenty years too young and we're all just acting like..."

"Would you hush your mouth?" Aunt Casey said, slamming down Mama's picture. "Who are you to talk anyway? You always got some girl tagging along after you and not one of them's older than nineteen. Why, I ought to have you arrested is what I ought to do."

Gigi jumped back in, accusing Aunt Casey of knowing about the lessons and yelling at Grandaddy Opal about their arrangement, and Miss Emmaline had a few loud words to say to Uncle Toole so that everyone was talking at once and no one was hearing anything. How could Mama and Dane return with all this commotion going on?

"Stop!" I yelled. "Everybody stop. You're messing up the vibrations. They're coming back and I can't hear. I can't feel. Just stop it!"

Everybody hushed but not because of me. The lights had gone out. Uncle Toole flicked on his lighter and lit some of the candle bottles. We all picked one up and moved to the center of the room. Outside was almost black and the sound of the wind whistled through the edges of the little pull-out window above Dane's desk. Then the sound grew louder and louder and Miss Emmaline began to sing again, competing with the thunderous noise outside, and when the whole house down to the foundation shook, I wasn't sure if it was the tornado hitting us or amazing grace.

Chapter 11

THE SOUND OF the tornado ripping Grandaddy Opal's house from its foundation and hurling the splintered pieces across the street left us deaf and stunned. Miss Emmaline Wilson had pushed me to the floor, and when the tornado struck, she was on top of me with her arms wrapped around me, holding on tight. I didn't think I'd ever want her to let go. It was a new experience being held like that, the way I figured Mama would have held me if she had lived, if she were there then. I knew right away Dane and Mama didn't make it. I knew something had gone wrong in the touchdown. I wanted to blame someone and I thought about Uncle Toole but he was curled up on the floor in a ball so tight we thought we were going to need one of Grandaddy Opal's carpentry tools to pry him open again.

Aunt Casey tried to get him to stand up or speak, but for a good long while he just stayed tight and wouldn't even look at her. The rest of us brushed ourselves off and examined our bodies and the basement for damage.

Water poured out of busted pipes and spread out over the floor, running toward Uncle Toole. Aunt Casey shouted at him to get up before he drowned. Uncle Toole lifted his head and said, "It's okay. It's okay, I'm alive."

"Well, of course it is, baby," Miss Emmaline said in a sweet, high-pitched voice that didn't sound like hers. Then she lowered it and said, "The Lord done saved your sorry soul 'cause you still got way too much learning to do. It's the good that die young, not folks like you."

I think we all expected Uncle Toole to start cussing at her and calling her names I wasn't supposed to hear, but he didn't. He cried and wagged his head and bit by bit his body unfolded. He stood up, the tears still streaming down his face, the jagged scar on his forehead pale and shiny from sweat. He held his thick-muscled arms straight out in front of him and walked toward Aunt Casey, looking stiff, like a mummy. We all backed away, everyone except Aunt Casey. She stood there and let him throw himself on her and beg her forgiveness for all the hurt he'd ever caused her. "I swear, babe, I'll make it up to you."

Aunt Casey, straining under the weight of his arms flung over her, pointed toward the sky. "Can't you see we got bigger problems than you to worry about right now?" she said. "Now, pull yourself together and help Opal out. I swear, of all the times to have some kind of conversion experience." Aunt Casey pushed him off her, but I could tell she was hopeful.

The steps leading upstairs had collapsed in the pressure of the house being sucked away. Dane's bookshelves had fallen over and most of the candle bottles were crushed beneath them.

Grandaddy Opal kicked his way through the debris and was on the other side of the room with Mr. Eugene Wadell, tugging at some big piece of something blocking the exit from the basement to the backyard. Gigi cheered them on. Finally they got the way clear enough for them to reach the door. Grandaddy Opal opened it and we burst through to the outside, relieved to find the world still there. I lifted my face to the rain and saw the sun trying to break through the silvery clouds.

Grandaddy Opal pointed to his garage. "Well look-a there, it's still standing! The tornado skipped right over it."

We all trudged up the slope of Grandaddy's backyard to the front of the garage. Miss Emmaline's car, the car Grandaddy Opal had been working on before the tornado hit, Uncle Toole's pickup, and Gigi's van were all still lined up in the driveway. Gigi declared she was grateful that for once she hadn't parked her van in front of the house. Mr. Eugene Wadell said it was because he was the one who had been driving. He was the one who had saved her car. He looked around at us all, I think expecting us to get down on our knees and thank him. Gigi took his hand and smiled, but the rest of us followed Grandaddy Opal out to the street to see what other damage had been done to the neighborhood.

Grandaddy Opal's house had been hit the worst but shingles and siding had been thrown all over the neighborhood, damaging other people's roofs and breaking windows. Most of his house landed on the lawns across the street, and that's where Grandaddy Opal headed. The rest of us trotted along behind him.

He jumped onto the heap that was his house and started picking through his belongings, picking up books and equipment and setting them in a pile to one side. People came out of their houses and joined us, and because Grandaddy Opal didn't say anything, neither did anyone else. They just climbed on top of the heap and pulled out anything they could. When they had an armload, they brought it across the street and set it in Grandaddy Opal's garage.

We all worked in that strange silence for almost an hour, digging and carrying and setting down, and digging some more. It felt as if we were still waiting for the storm, still tense, holding our breath. Then Grandaddy Opal jumped up and shouted, "Found them, by golly!"

We all looked up from our digging posts to see what he held above his head. It looked like three mashed boxes of typing paper held together with a piece of rope.

Then Gigi said, "His manuscripts! The original manuscripts. What are you doing with them?"

"He gave 'em to me, that's what," Grandaddy Opal said. He hopped off the house pile and marched back to his garage, hugging Dane's manuscripts in his arms. Then he flopped down in one of the rockers someone had carried over and had himself a heart attack.

Chapter 12

I HAD TO RIDE in the van with Gigi and Mr. Eugene
Wadell. We were the first ones behind the ambulance. Then came Aunt Casey and Uncle Toole, and
behind them Miss Emmaline Wilson.

Gigi kept real quiet in the van. She sat in the passenger seat next to Mr. Wadell and stared out the window. I didn't see her blink even once. Mr. Wadell told
her everything would be all right, and I wondered how
he knew.

Grandaddy Opal arrived at the emergency room a
good fifteen minutes before us, and a nurse said doctors
were already with him. We waited in the crowded waiting room. Gigi stood at the desk filling out forms, Mr.
Wadell had taken orders for sodas and was popping
money into the vending machine, and Uncle Toole and
Aunt Casey were standing in a corner real close to each
other talking sweet. I stood at the window and looked
out at all the cars in the parking lot. I tried to keep my
mind on the cars, on the lady carrying flowers hurrying

toward the building. I watched a bald-headed man leaving the hospital looking as if he, too, had once carried flowers to someone he loved and now looking lost without them to carry back out again. I tried to think about them, wonder about them, but my mind kept taking me back to my own troubles. What had happened? Why hadn't Mama and Dane come back? Why did Grandaddy Opal have a heart attack? What had I done? Would he die? Where would he go if he did die? Would he see Mama? What had I done wrong?

Maybe it was my will. Maybe my will wasn't strong enough. Maybe it was like what Gigi had said to me once back when she caught me with her Ouija board. She had grabbed it away from me and told me not to go getting into her stuff and calling on the dead without knowing what I was doing. Then she hid the Ouija board away. Is that what I had done? Had I called up the dead and messed it up somehow?

Maybe I had wanted Dane and Mama back so much that I willed them to try to come before they were ready. Maybe my will was strong enough to call on the tornado but not strong enough for Dane and Mama to return in one piece. Or maybe it was my dancing. The dancing started everyone fighting, got Grandaddy Opal upset, stirred things up. I shouldn't have danced; it confused things, confused Mama and Dane.

I heard Miss Emmaline Wilson behind me. "Why don't you come sit by me, angel?"

I turned around. She was sitting on a couch and patting the seat beside her.

I hesitated. Maybe it was her holding on to me

down there in that basement, blocking me so Dane and Mama couldn't even see me there. Maybe it was me loving her voice and her protecting me, loving the soft way her body pressed against mine.

"It's going to be all right," she said, same as Mr. Wadell.

What would I do without Grandaddy Opal?

"Don't you worry, he'll be all right," Miss Emmaline said, as if I'd asked the question out loud. "That man rides his bicycle miles every day. Why, my house is more than five miles from his, and he rides to there and back and still has energy to turn cartwheels. He'll be all right, you'll see. We just have to wait through this bad time, that's all."

I lifted my head, startled. "Dane used to say that," I said.

"Dane?"

I nodded. "Dane used to say, 'I just got to wait through this bad time. Just wait it out, and things will be all right.'"

Miss Emmaline Wilson patted the seat beside her again. "That's right, angel, we'll wait through the bad times together. Come on and sit down beside me."

I sat down and let her take my hand in hers. I didn't know how cold my hand was until she took it and massaged it. I didn't know the joints ached.

I pretended she wasn't holding it. I pretended I wasn't there. That's what I should have done in the basement. I should have ignored everything but the storm. We all should have. We weren't concentrating. That was the answer. I needed to wait until Dane gave

me a sign that it was all right to be with Miss Emmaline. But then maybe her saying we had to wait through
the bad times was the sign. Maybe.

I remembered how I used to hear Dane pacing in
his cave and talking to himself. He'd say the same thing
about waiting through the bad times, and I'd hear him
tearing up his papers, whatever he had been working
on. Once even, I thought I heard him crying.

I shifted closer to Miss Emmaline and she put her
arm around my shoulders. I could smell her sweet perfume, like lily flowers. I closed my eyes and pretended
Mama was holding me. It was probably all right if I
thought it was Mama. If things had worked out right,
if I had done it right, it would have been her holding
me just that way, and Dane would be pacing the hospital floor waiting for news of his daddy and saying we
just got to wait through this bad time. Mama and Dane,
Dane and Mama, where were they? What's going to
happen to Grandaddy Opal—and me?

Mr. Eugene Wadell came over with our drinks and
handed them to us.

"I think if we could get together in a circle and focus
on Mr. McCloy's heart and circulatory system—I
mean, if we could just visualize healing..." Mr.
Wadell's voice trailed off and he looked around for Gigi.

"Prayer, you mean," said Miss Emmaline.

"Uh—" Mr. Wadell pulled open his can of Sprite
and took a sip.

Gigi came up behind him. "No," she said. "It's more
like a séance where you visualize the person you're trying to contact, only this time we'll be contacting Opal's

heart and telling it to start beating again." She looked at Mr. Wadell. "But I don't think Opal would want..."

Miss Emmaline stood, pulling me up with her. "Honey, if it ain't beating by now, he's long dead."

Aunt Casey and Uncle Toole heard her and rushed over to us. "He's dead?" they both said, looking at all our faces for the answer.

The doctor answered them. He had come up behind us, looking tired and grizzled as if he had been on duty for days. He sighed with his words when he spoke. "Mr. McCloy's fine."

"Praise the Lord," said Miss Emmaline.

The doctor turned to her and spoke as if it were just the two of them standing there.

"It was a mild attack, but of course we'll keep him here a few days for observation. If you want to see him, check at the information station and they'll give you his room number." Then he bowed to her and left.

Grandaddy Opal was awake when we came into his room. He had an IV needle stuck in his hand and an oxygen tube running into his nose. He looked pale, and even his hair looked sick, all matted down against his head and face, but his eyes were open and alert.

"Well, well, well," he said, lifting his free hand off the bed a little.

I hurried to his side. I wanted to be in front of the others and not pushed out of the way. I wanted to see him. Gigi stood on his other side and didn't say anything.

I touched his arm, and he took my hand. His hand was cold like mine, and shaking; his hands were always shaking. He told me once it was because he drank too much cola, but Gigi said he had nerve problems. Was that why he'd had a heart attack?

"Miracle." Grandaddy Opal's voice was hoarse. He removed the oxygen tube from his nose and coughed, then replaced it.

"I'm sorry," I said.

"Hooey! We're all okay, ain't we?"

I shrugged.

"Well, sure we are. It ain't like you had anything to do with it. Now," he looked at the others, "how long am I supposed to stay in this here hoosegow?"

"Just a few days, I think," Miss Emmaline said. Gigi stayed quiet and studied the IV needle going into Grandaddy Opal's hand.

"And then what? Have you thought about where we're all going to stay? Y'all been talking it over?"

"We're heading home in the morning," Uncle Toole said, squeezing Aunt Casey with his arm around her shoulder. "Once we're sure you're okay and all, I mean."

"Opal, you can stay with me for a while," Miss Emmaline said. Uncle Toole let out a hoot. She ignored him. "Miracle and Gigi, too."

"Miracle isn't staying with you or him," Gigi said, stirring herself and backing away from the bed. "All this behind-my-back doings with the dancing lessons. No, we'll go stay with Mrs. Hewlett, that way I can be close by for my Other Realms meetings. And if she doesn't have room in her home, we'll stay at her gift shop." Gigi twisted around to look for Mr. Wadell. He was standing by the door drinking down his Sprite and staring out into the hallway.

Then Grandaddy Opal said to me, "Girlie, run on and get me a Coke, my mouth is desert dry."

I lifted the unopened Coke can I held in my other hand. "You can have mine," I said.

"Nah, I want one of them." His eyes shifted to the doorway and Mr. Wadell's can of Sprite. "Get me one of them."

I looked around at everyone, then back to Grandaddy Opal. "But will they let you . . ."

"I don't care what they'll let me do or not. Get me one of them danged sodas!"

Gigi handed me some money, and I handed her my Coke and ran out of the room. I knew when I got back everything would be decided. I feared Gigi and I would end up staying with Mr. Eugene Wadell, and I had the sneaking suspicion that he lived with his ninety-year-old mama who still helped him get dressed every morning. He always wore his pants belted way up over his jiggly waist and his shirt looked like his mama tucked him in real good every day before he stepped out the door. Besides that, I didn't trust him. Even though Grandaddy Opal seemed to be okay, I wasn't so sure he could predict the future. I had the feeling everything was not going to turn out all right the way he said it would.

Aunt Casey once said the channeling and mystic vibrations he was always feeling were phony baloney, and I agreed. She said Mr. Wadell just hung around Gigi to pick up her secrets. "He thinks she's got a bag of tricks stored away somewhere and he wants at it," she said. "Wait till he finds out she's for real."

Then Uncle Toole had said, "No, wait till Gigi finds out he's a phony, then we'll see the gunpowder fly."

I dropped the money in the soda machine and pressed the Sprite button. On the way back, I imagined what it would be like to live with Miss Emmaline all the time. I pictured her living in a broom-swept house, with everything in its proper place and all her furniture stuffed fat with feathers. I pictured her singing while she cooked, the rich-smelling sauces and gravies bubbling and dancing merrily in their pots.

It was real quiet when I got back to the room. Everyone turned to look at me. I brushed past them and set Grandaddy Opal's soda on his bedside table. He looked at it as if it were arsenic. When I turned around, Aunt Casey was there holding her hands out to me. She had just put on a fresh coat of red lipstick, red for fire and rage, and she was smiling at me with such a funny smile, a fake, distorted smile, it scared me. I backed away from her.

"Well now," she said, her voice pitched high and strange, "what do you think about staying with your aunt Casey, girl? Won't that be a hoot? Why, it'll be just like a slumber party."

Aunt Casey kept smiling and Uncle Toole joined her, wrapping his arm back around her shoulder like he was thinking of having it glued there.

"You, me, and Gigi?" I asked.

Gigi and Grandaddy Opal exchanged a look, and I knew I was going alone. I nodded my head. I understood. They knew it was all my fault.

Chapter 13

I SAID GOOD-BYE to Grandaddy Opal the next afternoon. He was sitting up in his hospital bed looking more like himself without the tube running up his nose. Miss Emmaline sat in a chair next to him.

"Hey, girl," he said, "I ain't contagious, come up close where I can see you."

I inched closer and leaned against his bed, touching the blanket right near his hand.

"You got Etain with you?"

I shook my head. "I didn't know I could take her with me."

" 'Course you can. You think I'm going to ride her? Now you have Casey and Toole stop by the garage and pick her up, you hear?"

"Yes, sir."

Miss Emmaline stood up and patted my shoulder. "You'll come see us, won't you?"

"Yes, ma'am," I said.

Grandaddy Opal tapped his hand on the bedside

rail. "Hey, it ain't permanent. Once I get me a new house built, we'll be back together again, same as always."

Gigi said almost the same thing when I said goodbye to her.

I met her back at Grandaddy Opal's place. She was in the garage picking up the bits and pieces that were hers.

"This will just be for a few weeks," she had said. "Just till things get settled. Here's Mrs. Hewlett's number in case you need anything, and you have the gift shop number, don't you?"

"Yes."

"Now, you make sure you come see me often and wear your purple. You make sure you wear your purple. I'll send you some money and you go shopping and get yourself some new things. I'll make sure to send you extra for your birthday. My gift—all this stuff's ruined." She waved her hand at our belongings stacked in wet piles in the garage.

I turned my head and searched the piles, thinking I'd see her gift crushed and wet and wrapped in Mrs. Hewlett's trademark angels wrapping paper—an idea suggested by the late Mr. Hewlett through Gigi. I saw Dane's bathrobe instead, and as soon as Gigi had said her final good-byes, I ran over to the pile of wet clothes, pulled out the robe, and wore it shivering in the back of Uncle Toole's pickup all the way to Alabama.

The last time I'd been in Uncle Toole and Aunt Casey's house had been about two months before Dane melted. It had been Uncle Toole's birthday and we were having a pig roast in their backyard with all of Uncle

Toole's mover buddies. Dane had stayed in the house with Gigi and some of the other women who were cooking the butter beans and collards and other vegetables. He claimed he no longer ate pig and sat in a chair in the corner writing stuff down in the notepad he carried with him whenever he left the house. Gigi told him it wasn't the pig keeping him in the house but the company. She said he had always just naturally preferred the company of women. He slammed down his notepad and said if she wanted to know the truth, he preferred no company at all, especially hers. Then he stormed out of the house and sat in the van in one-hundred-degree heat and refused to come back in the house.

Nothing had changed in Uncle Toole and Aunt Casey's house since that last visit. The stale odor of cigarettes still permeated the house—the curtains, the carpets, the furniture, the clothes, even the dishes. My first glass of water brought it all back. Everything tasted like ash.

The living room and dining room were still jammed with Uncle Toole's junk, stuff people moving out of their homes no longer wanted. They gave him broken fans and heaters, and toasters and televisions. Chairs with their backs broken off and sofas with the stuffing popping out like newly sprouting bolls of cotton were all heaped together, waiting for repair. I saw the familiar pile of shoes—Aunt Casey's same old high heels in silver and gold and shiny black and white, and Uncle Toole's same old work boots, all of them clumped together just outside the hall closet. The only thing different at all was the mess on the kitchen table. It used

117

to be cluttered with old newspapers and the Confederate mugs and dishes and miniature cannons Uncle Toole had collected. These had been moved to the countertops to make room for Aunt Casey's psychology course work. Now the table was covered with books and papers, a typewriter, and a giant overflowing Confederate ashtray.

They gave me Aunt Casey's wig room for a bedroom. She kept all her sewing and cutting supplies on a long table that looked just like the one at the back of my old dance studio—the one at the church with the thirty-two-cup coffee pot on it. She kept her wigs on plastic heads that lined the shelves across from the broken-backed couch that became my bed. The wig heads had no faces, just indentations where the eyes should be and a mound where the nose was supposed to be and no mouth at all. At night those heads stared at me, watched me sleeping, whispered nightmares into my ears. I didn't sleep much anymore. I figured it was only for a few weeks. I could go without sleep for a few weeks. But those weeks turned into months and I was still struggling to sleep, still in Alabama, still living with Aunt Casey and Uncle Toole.

In school, I got in trouble for erasing my name off the blackboard. The English teacher had put our names in groups up on the board. I was in the Wednesday group. On Wednesday, my group had to read their short stories to the class. I didn't like seeing my name up there, separate from me. I didn't like going home knowing that my name was still there on the blackboard, and I feared returning to school in the morning and finding my name gone. I erased my name. I took it back. The English teacher put it back up. I erased it again, and he sent a note home to Aunt Casey.

Aunt Casey was too busy. She worked all day at her beauty salon and went to college three nights a week. When she was home she was either arguing with Uncle Toole or in my room sewing on her wigs. I couldn't bother her.

I gave the note to Uncle Toole. Ever since the tornado, he spent his free nights lying on his bed watching TV and looking like some kind of vice dispenser. He always had a beer resting on his chest and a spare cigarette in his belly button for when he stubbed out the one hanging in his mouth into the empty beer can resting in the pit of his arm. He could spend hours smoking and drinking and pushing on the TV set's remote control buttons.

Uncle Toole read the note.

"Says here you're erasing your name off the blackboard."

"That's right."

"So?"

I shrugged, and he shook his head.

"Go find me a pen so's I can sign this thing."

I brought him my pen and he wrote at the bottom of the note, "So What!!!" and signed it.

I gave my English teacher the note before I went home that afternoon, and I erased my name. I heard the teacher sighing behind me. The next day was Wednesday and my name was back on the board. The teacher had me read my story first. I had written a story about a ballerina who loved to do pirouettes. She did them all the time—morning, noon, and night—and she got so good at doing them and so fast that she began to spin like a tornado. She spun so fast she couldn't stop. She got thinner and thinner until she was as thin as a needle. Still she spun because she couldn't stop. She spun until she disappeared.

The teacher reminded me that the story was supposed to be about a fantasy vacation not just a fantasy, and I told him it *was* about a fantasy vacation. The kids laughed.

At the end of the class, the English teacher erased my name off the board. He just rubbed it out, took it away. I asked him to put it back up so that I could erase it. He refused and told me he had had enough of my nonsense. I stopped signing my name on all my papers after that and the teachers gave me zeros. They said they would give me a real grade if I signed my name and turned the papers back in. Zero is a real grade. I didn't sign my name. At the end of the year I got all incompletes on my report card. I didn't show it to Uncle Toole or Aunt Casey and they never asked to see it.

UNCLE TOOLE wanted a baby. That's what their latest fights were all about. That's all they talked and argued about. Uncle Toole said the tornado had made everything clear to him. He said we all could have died. He wanted a baby to carry on the Dawsey name.

At night, he followed Aunt Casey from room to room, even coming into my room, if that's where Aunt Casey had settled, and argued again and again about having children. And every time they argued I closed my eyes and drifted away to my safe place, the place with the green fields and butterfly blanket. The place where I used to talk to Dane. He wasn't there anymore; his voice had gone. I knew he felt too disappointed in me to speak and that my trying to bring him and Mama back, willing them to appear on my thirteenth birthday—and thirteen a very bad luck number—only sent Gigi and Grandaddy Opal away, and Dane and Mama were no closer to me. I'd lost them all. All I had left were Aunt Casey and Uncle Toole, and they were fighting about having children.

"Children!" I remember Aunt Casey shouting, breaking into my fairy dream. "What do I need with children? I've already got one child, and I'm not talking about Miracle. Besides, you know we agreed long ago we weren't going to have any children, that I had done all the raising up I was going to do."

"But come on, babe, every woman wants a little bundle to cuddle. It ain't natural not to," Uncle Toole had whined.

"You're saying I'm not normal? Don't try reverse psychology on me. Anyways, as soon as I have a baby tying me to the house, you'll be off again, same as usual. I know you, Toole Dawsey, you'll be bored and restless in no time. Bored and restless, bored and restless, that's your middle name."

Aunt Casey was right, too. He could never sit still. Even when he was lying on the bed watching TV, he could never stay on one channel for more than a couple of minutes, and he was always fussing with his beer cans and tearing at his cigarette pack. Aunt Casey told him he had attention deficit disorder and if they had a baby, the baby would more than likely have it, too. She read to him all about it from one of her psychology books, pointing out that the person in the case study ran red lights all the time just the way he did, but Uncle Toole didn't listen. He was too busy picking out food grime from between the slats in the kitchen table with a toothpick.

Aunt Casey said he needed to be on medication. She'd gotten to thinking just about everybody needed to be on medication. She said Grandaddy Opal could use some Valium or something to calm him down. "He's so hyper. He's an itch," she said. "He's just an itch."

She said I needed Prozac. "You must have chronic depression," she told me once in front of Mrs. Beane, who had come for her final wig fitting.

"You never talk anymore. You're like a ghost drifting around this house. Really, I never know what you're thinking. You used to talk. You used to stick your tongue out at me, remember? When you were younger?" She shook her head and patted Mrs. Beane's new hair.

"What do you think?" She held a mirror above the back of Mrs. Beane's head so she could see how it looked.

"I don't really know her, but she does look awful thin and pale. And her hair's a bit peculiar, isn't it?"

"I meant *your* hair," Aunt Casey said.

"Oh, yes, it fits much better." Mrs. Beane turned to me. "What do you think, dear?"

I looked up from the book I was reading. I studied Mrs. Beane's face. She reminded me of one of the wig heads, one of the shiny plastic heads with indentations where the eyes should go and a mound for the nose and no mouth at all. I didn't want to tell her this, I didn't want to tell her I could already see her astral and physical bodies separating, that she wasn't going to make it, she wouldn't survive her cancer. I didn't want to look at her anymore or think about her. I tried to say something nice, but when I opened my mouth nothing came out.

Aunt Casey turned Mrs. Beane around. "See what I mean? She didn't used to be like this. She used to have some life in her. She used to always be jumping around on the furniture, asking Dane—that's her father—to watch. 'Dane, Dane, look-it, Dane,' " she said, imitating me. " 'Look. Dane, look. Dane, Dane, watch this.' " She turned to see if I was listening.

I was.

"I think purple depresses you," she said, taking up her scissors and cutting some invisible hairs from the bottom of the wig. "Gigi's not here, why not try some red or green—or pink. Pink's a pretty color. And you could grow your hair back out and I'd buy you hair ribbons—pinks and reds and greens, plaids even. Don't you think pink would be pretty on her, Mrs. Beane?"

I stayed in the purple. Purple was spiritual, purple was power. Purple protected me from the wig heads that had no faces, and from cancer, and from the dark. I had grown afraid of the dark, of what might be waiting for me there. I put on Dane's bathrobe, over the purple—a double shield.

Chapter 14

THAT SUMMER, Gigi went to Greece with Mr.
Eugene Wadell and married him, standing in the
ruins of an ancient cathedral near the Sanctuary of
Asklepios. I didn't know she had gone until Aunt
Casey handed me a letter from her, saying how she
guessed Gigi had discovered Mr. Eugene Wadell's one
good trait: He had a lot of money.

I took the letter to my room and read it with my
back to the wig heads.

Miracle,

*It's ridiculous that Casey didn't tell you all this about
me going to Greece and getting married. By the time you
get this letter we'll have been here forever, and I'll be an
old married lady, but Casey, the psychologist, insisted I
tell you myself, so now you know. We got married in these
ancient ruins under some lovely pine trees, at least I think
they were pine. The whole place is a sanctuary to the
Greek god-physician Asklepios, and way back when,*

patients would sleep in the building called the abaton
where the god would visit them in their dreams and
miraculously cure them. It's very exciting! Some of the
stories of the miracles and magic cures were carved into
the stones here. Well, Eugene and I held a séance and
contacted the ancient god and he has given us the healing
powers. I have been visited by him several times in my
dreams. When we get back to the States (that's how they
say it here when you're talking about going home), we're
going to have our own sanctuary done up like the pictures
of the one here. Not the Gymnasium, or some of the other
buildings, but we'll have healing baths and the abaton
where you sleep and receive the healing visitations. So,
how about that? How about your old Gigi getting
married?

I'm sending you something real special in the mail. It
may not arrive for months, who knows, it's got to get all
the way from Greece to Alabama! Now you know what's
going on.

Gigi

After I read the letter, Aunt Casey came into my
room. She sat down at the wig table and picked up the
blond wig with the needle and thread dangling from the
underside and said, "So did she tell you?"

"That she got married? Yes."

"Anyway, isn't it a kicker? Gigi married. And who
would have thought that little phony was rich."

"What's he do?" I asked.

"Do? I don't think he does anything. Maybe he won
the lottery, or maybe he stole it, I don't know."

"When's Gigi coming back? When will I move back in with her and Grandaddy Opal?"

"Miracle," Aunt Casey said, pausing with the needle in one hand and the wig balanced on the other. "We need to have us a heart-to-heart." She poked the needle into the wig's cap and pulled the thread through. I folded Gigi's letter back into its envelope and waited.

"It's just that now Gigi's married she'll be living with that Eugene Wadell. He's got a place in Tennessee."

"Tennessee?"

Aunt Casey held up the wig and examined it, peering into the underside as if she were about to put it on her face. "Yeah, Tennessee." She came out from behind the wig. "Come on, you're thirteen, you know how it is. She's a newlywed. She needs to be alone with her hubby."

I shrugged. "I know. It's okay. Grandaddy Opal and I can do all right on our own. We were really on our own before anyway. His house will be ready soon, I bet, and we..."

Aunt Casey shook her head. "There's a lot of red tape with insurance and all. His house, who knows when they'll get around to that, and anyway, it's been decided, you'll just stay on with us."

Aunt Casey's face went back into the wig and I just sat there on my bed, the bed that was really a sofa, only Uncle Toole or somebody sawed the back off of it. I stuck the letter in the pocket of my robe and stood up.

"Okay," I said. "I'm going to go ride Etain."

"Good. Good idea." Aunt Casey popped out from behind the wig and smiled, and for once there wasn't any lipstick stuck to her teeth.

I lost Gigi's letter on that ride with Etain. I don't know how. It must have fallen out of the pocket of Dane's robe. The wind must have carried it off somewhere.

We didn't talk about Gigi or her marriage or Tennessee all summer. I didn't talk much at all that summer because there was no one around to talk to. Uncle Toole's moving business was so busy he never got in till late at night, sometimes after midnight even, and then he'd have to get up at six the next day and load up another van all over again. He came home tired and dirty and moaning.

Aunt Casey had decided to go for a degree in psychology instead of just taking random courses in it, and every spare minute she had was spent down at the university. She had even begun to dress differently. Instead of spandex and tight sparkly shirts, she wore baggy jeans and extra large tee shirts and socks and flat wide sandals that had no back strap and kept flying off her feet. She had to learn a whole new way of walking. Her hair was combed down, too, less stiff, and she kept it dyed red and wore almost no makeup. She reminded me of Susan, my old dance teacher.

I asked Aunt Casey about taking dancing lessons again since I was going to be living with them, and she went white in the face and said I'd better not.

I danced anyway. No one was home. I taught myself. Every day I danced, slow quiet dances, movement without music. I couldn't play any music because I had to listen in case Dane had forgiven me and wanted to speak to me again. I decided he must have gone back in time, found Mama, and the two of them had passed through one of those wormholes Grandaddy Opal had talked about. One of the wormholes that you could pass through and into a parallel universe. That's where they were, living in a parallel universe and waiting for me to find my way to them. Of course, I wasn't sure. Last time I had been *so* sure. I had to be careful, certain, so I waited, and danced, and listened.

I stopped dancing at night, when it got dark. If no one else was home, I turned on all the lights and sat on the kitchen counter drinking sweet tea and counting to ten thousand. As long as someone came home before I reached ten thousand I knew I was safe. I still didn't know why I was so frightened, so afraid of the dark, as if the darkness mirrored something hidden, dangerous, but dancing and counting kept me safe.

We were always going to go see Grandaddy Opal one of these days but that day never came. I spoke to him on the phone a few times, but he seemed distracted, and it was as if he had to force himself to sound happy to be talking to me. He never called me, and I stopped calling him after a while because I understood. I knew he blamed me for trying to bring Mama and Dane back too soon. He blamed me for his heart attack. I rode Etain a lot that summer, riding farther and farther away from home each time. I read the newspaper every day and cut out any miracle stories I found and glued them in my new notebook. I made my own meals out of what we had in the house: spaghetti with salad dressing, Frosted Mini-Wheats in beer, mayonnaise sandwiches, and sometimes wild cherry tomatoes picked from a one-time garden in the back of the house, but they gave me diarrhea. Then school started up again and Gigi's package arrived from Greece.

It was leaning against the front door of the house when Etain and I rode home from my first day at school. I brought it to my bedroom and set it down on Aunt Casey's wig table to open it. Beneath the brown paper wrapping was a box with a letter taped to the top. I tore it off and read it.

Miracle,

The Greeks are full of the knowledge of magic and the supernatural. I found this old book of love potions and magic ceremonies in a musty, dusty bookstore underneath a pile of Life magazines, of all things. The book is in Greek, but the pictures are great. Thought you might be interested. The shawl, of course, is to wear. So that's all from this happily married lady—

Gigi

The book was written in Greek just as Gigi had said, and the strange letters made the idea of love potions seem more magical and exciting. The pictures were pen-and-ink drawings of plants and bugs used, I guessed, in the potions. The shawl was silk, dyed a deep purple with shiny gold threads running through it, outlining the shape of a giant red bird. The tassels that ran around the edges of the shawl were made of tiny silver and gold beads on loops of gold thread. I doubled the shawl over so it made a triangle and wrapped it around my shoulders. It felt heavy and the tip of the triangle came all the way down to the backs of my knees. I decided to wear it to school.

I knew everyone in school would stare at me in my shawl, but one girl, Mary Louise Pickard, a popular girl who usually traveled in a pack of other girls, stopped me in the hallway and said, "Cool, where'd you get it?"

She moved around me the way Grandaddy Opal did years ago when I had fallen down the stairs, and I felt a tingling buzz of excitement shoot through my body and spill across my chest. It was hard to breathe, the pleasure was so great.

A couple of Mary Louise's friends also stopped to stare.

"Is that real gold?" one of them asked.

"Yes."

"Aren't you afraid of getting it stolen? I don't think I'd wear it to school," said Mary Louise.

"No, it has an ancient curse on it," I said, feeling the buzz rush up to my head and flash behind my eyes. "It can only be given away, never stolen, or the person who stole it will die a terrible death."

"Really?" the group said, looking at one another.

"Oh, yes. It's from Greece, which is just full of curses."

"What's it do?"

"Huh?" I turned around to face another girl, another stranger.

"Like, is it supposed to be magic, or something?"

"Oh, my grandmother gave it to me—uh, passed it down to me. I come from a long line of mediums and healers and clairvoyants. The shawl is—is used for love ceremonies."

"Love ceremonies!" several of the girls said at the same time, and their voices were pitched higher than before. They moved in closer to me, and Mary Louise asked me what kind of love ceremonies, but the bell rang and I couldn't answer; we were all late for our classes.

After school, while I was unlocking Etain from the bike rack, some of the girls came back up to me and asked about the ceremonies. By then I had had time to think. I told them how each generation of women in my family had one of the supernatural talents. My grandmother could contact the dead, my mother could see into the future, and I could cast love spells, spells that would make someone fall in love with you.

The girls were laughing and their voices got high and squeally again. They had turned to each other, ignoring me and talking about Cash Franklin, the hottest guy in school. One of the girls mentioned another boy's name and they all laughed, imagining him under their spell. More girls gathered around me and they told one another who they wanted for their "love punkin" and laughed some more and pretended to be under a spell themselves, and some of them missed their bus but they didn't care.

Etain and I stood at the center of the crowd almost forgotten and then someone asked, "But what if more than one person likes the same guy? Then what?"

Everyone got quiet and turned to me, waiting for my answer.

I tightened my shawl, making a double knot, keeping my fingers busy and trying to think fast. My knees were shaking. "Oh, well," I said, still busy with the knot,

"I do a spell that only lasts a couple of weeks, and whoever comes to me first gets the spell. Because, uh, in order to make the spell permanent, the guy who's under the spell must come to me and request the girl who put him under the spell. If he does that, then it becomes permanent, but permanent means forever, so I'm very careful about doing permanent spells. Permanent can be a disaster." I tried to give them a knowing look to show them I had had plenty of experience with disasters.

They asked me more questions, like how long does it take for the spell to work, and when could I do it, and could I do it there in school? The questions were all coming so fast I couldn't think, and I was getting scared. I pushed Etain through the crowd of girls and said I had to get home, that we'd talk some other time, and the girls let me go.

Then, after I'd climbed on Etain, before I pedaled away, I saw a girl standing under a tree just beyond the crowd. She was watching me, and it made something inside me squeeze up tight. She reminded me of the wig heads watching me at home.

Chapter 15

I COULD FIND NOWHERE to hide, nowhere I felt safe. That was the problem with Aunt Casey and Uncle Toole's house. They didn't have a basement, a cave I could tuck myself into surrounded by Dane's books. I couldn't hide in my bedroom with all those wig heads watching me all the time, keeping me awake at night. I couldn't even hide in the bathtub because they didn't have one, just a shower stall with an old mildewed shower curtain hanging from it. The curtain felt slimy and smelled bad the way Etain's saddle did whenever it got wet.

I needed to hide. I knew those girls at school would expect me to cast spells and give them potions. I knew they'd be waiting for me when I went to school the next morning. I wanted to hide under the covers in my bed and never come out. I took off my shawl and put on Dane's robe and climbed onto my bed. I closed my eyes and strained to get to my fairyland, but even that had disappeared—melted. I blamed it on the wig heads.

They were waiting for me, lined up on the shelf, laughing their nasty laugh. "What do *you* know about love?"

I got under the covers, but I could feel the wig heads behind me, wanting an answer, waiting for my answer. I curled up tight, barely breathing, sweating beneath so many covers. What did I know about love? Why did I tell all those girls I could cast love spells? Why not contacting the dead or reading auras or palms even? I couldn't breathe. I threw off the covers, gasping for air. I sat up and faced the wig heads. "I don't believe in love," I told them. "It's not real. It's not a live thing." I stood up and went to the shelves. "That's what I know. I know all about it. I'm wiser than anybody. I'm an expert on love because I know the truth—there's no such thing." I turned one of the heads around so just the back of the wig faced me. "You can't touch it, can you?" I turned another one around. "You can't hold it in your hand, can you? Can you? Can you?" I turned them all around, facing away from me. "Love is make-believe. It's all make-believe, and I can make believe I'm the world's greatest spell caster. So what do you think about that?"

The wig heads didn't answer.

"I didn't think so. You're not real. You can't watch me or tell me anything."

I stayed up all night reading the book of spells Gigi sent me, and it didn't matter that I couldn't read Greek. I studied the words, the shapes of the letters, and I studied the picture on the page opposite the words and a feeling would come over me. Each page left me with a different feeling, a different idea for casting spells and creating potions. And while I read and turned myself into the world's greatest spell caster, Uncle Toole and Aunt Casey were in their bedroom across the hall, fighting.

Uncle Toole claimed Aunt Casey wasn't the woman he had married anymore. He said she'd changed and he didn't like the change one single bit. He said there wasn't one sexy thing about her left now that she was all into the college life, and her head was filled with so much garbage there wasn't any room for him.

Aunt Casey said Uncle Toole hadn't changed enough. She said he was stuck in adolescence, refusing to grow up, and she knew for a fact he hadn't been just working too hard lately. She said he was up to his old tricks, and that's when Uncle Toole said, "That just shows what you know. I have too changed, you just aren't around enough anymore to notice."

They slammed a lot of doors back and forth and Uncle Toole had to sleep in the living room on one of his busted-up sofas. Love wasn't real. If they just realized that, if they could just understand that very simple thing, they'd never fight again.

MARY LOUISE and her friends waited until lunchtime before coming up to me. I had my shawl on and I carried an old sewing bag of Aunt Casey's filled with plants and a few dead bugs I'd collected on my way to school. They found me waiting in the cafeteria line and they pulled me out of it.

"Forget about lunch," Mary Louise said. "Come on, we're going to my office."

Her office was underneath the bleachers that lined the quarter-mile track overgrown with grass and weeds, back behind the school. She said almost no one ever came down there during lunch unless it was to see her or one of the other girls in her group.

"I'm going to go first," she said. "If it works, then the rest of us will give you their business. If it doesn't work..."

"No! It works like this," I said. I couldn't let her take over, tell me what to do. This was mine.

"I choose who gets the spell. There are all kinds of curses if it's not done right. It has to be done right. I have to receive a message from—from Asklepios. Asklepios chooses the person. And there is a payment."

"I knew it," one of the girls said. "I told you it costs. What a racket."

"Yes," I nodded. "You must bring me one empty wine bottle and one white unused candle exactly seven inches long."

"That's what it costs? No money?" Mary Louise asked.

"No money. Now, I brought one candle bottle with me today for the first spell, but after this you must bring me the candle and the bottle, or the spell I cast today will be broken and you will never know love again."

"So, so who's that Ask—Aski person going to choose?" Mary Louise was bouncing on the balls of her feet, anxious to get on with it.

"Asklepios," I said. I sat down on the grass and crossed my legs in front of me. "I must contact the great god of all wisdom in love. Everyone sit down and hold hands around me."

The girls formed a circle around me and held hands. I closed my eyes and hummed and swayed the way Gigi always did. I hummed louder. I could feel the warm bodies of the girls around me. Around *me*! I concentrated. I thought about Mary Louise, the prettiest, the leader, and that other girl, quieter, not as pretty but nice looking. Boys would like her. I would choose her.

I opened my eyes and pointed at the girl. They said her name was Cara. I told her to sit in front of me, and I reached into my bag and pulled out the candle bottle and a small pocket mirror I'd found in the kitchen one day that past summer when I was making myself a lunch of hot dogs and Cheez Whiz. I was still afraid of mirrors. Gigi said mirrors could rob you of your soul. She said she used to contact the dead through mirror gazing, before she became an expert and didn't need mirrors anymore. It scared me to think of my soul being robbed, or worse, discovering I had no soul at all. I still never looked in mirrors, but I told Cara to stare into the pocket mirror and think of her true love. All the girls giggled when I said the words "true love." I gave them a serious look and they hushed.

I lit the candle bottle and told Cara to keep looking in the mirror and to imagine her true love gazing back at her. I held the candle bottle above her head and asked for her true love's name.

She turned red in the face and looked around at the other girls. I reminded her to keep gazing in the mirror. I asked her again, and she said his name was Justice Lee Halley.

I circled the bottle above her head and chanted the magic words: Kambok, Lovage Zweibach Zim Cara, Koombek Levege Zweindol Zim Justice. Then I set the candle bottle down by her feet and danced around her the way I had wanted to do for Gigi. I recited the words again, only louder this time and then again but softer, then softer. I did my old melting dance in front of the candle bottle and Cara, and I heard one of the other girls whisper, "She's a real professional."

I smiled inside myself and kept melting. They were all watching me, just the way I used to imagine it would be. I melted all the way down into the ground and lay still for so long someone asked if I was all right. I sat right up, clapped five times—five being the number of love and marriage and fire—and blew out the candle. I told Cara to hold her hand over the rising smoke and recite Justice's name five times. Then I dug back into my bag and pulled out a plastic sandwich bag filled with five blades of grass, five leaves from a dogwood tree, one dead cockroach, and a branch from an azalea bush.

"Gross, what's this for?" Cara asked.

"In order for the spell to work," I said, "Justice has to unknowingly carry the things in this bag home with him, but only after you have touched each object and said the words 'Zim Cara, Zim Justice' five times."

"I have to touch the cockroach? No way."

I adjusted my shawl. "Suit yourself, then." I started gathering my things together.

"Okay, okay. I've gone this far."

Cara took the bag, and all the girls gathered back around and examined the goodies I had collected.

The bell rang then and the group of us ran back toward the building. It was the first time I ever ran when the group behind me wasn't chasing me, and I smiled inside myself.

Chapter 16

MY SPELL WORKED! Justice Lee Halley invited Cara Johnson to the first dance of the school year.

After that, girls throughout the whole middle school wanted me to cast spells, and undo spells, and redo spells, and it didn't seem to matter that the spells failed as often as they worked. I collected so many candle bottles it was getting hard to hide them all in my room. I never ate lunch anymore, and I was always late getting home from school because of my new business. By the middle of the year, word of my abilities as a love magician reached the high school and I began to get their business as well. Everyone knew me, knew my name. I was Miracle, the love magician. It was wonderful to hear people call my name without having eggs and rocks hidden behind their backs. It was fun saying things that I knew no one understood, but because I was the love magician, they all laughed as if I had told a joke. It was fun when the girls all did what I said. If I said they had to sleep out in a tree in front of their beloved's house all night, they did it. If I said they had to sing a love song in the boys' bathroom, they did it, and it seemed that they had so much fun wondering what I would ask and watching others do silly things, it didn't matter whether the spells worked or not.

Then it all changed. It all turned sour, bit by bit. I had decided I wanted the girls to invite me over, let me go to their parties. I wanted them to call me up on the telephone. Every day before I left for home I'd say to someone, "Now you call me up, okay? You have my number? Don't lose it, it's not listed in the directory. Call me, okay?"

They always said they would, but no one did. Then I made it part of the instructions for one of my spells. Tilly Ann had to call me and speak to me for fifteen minutes if she wanted Timmy Riggs to be hers. Tilly Ann called me, and I could tell she was nervous. She asked me what she was supposed to say to me for fifteen minutes. I told her to say whatever it was she said to her other girlfriends. Tilly Ann just giggled and hung up. She had been on the phone with me for twenty-nine seconds.

That's when I realized the truth. None of the girls liked me. They were afraid of me. They never spoke to me except in a group and only during lunch or after school, and only about love potions. No one else ever called me up on the telephone, or rode home with me, or spent their Saturday afternoons with me. I didn't know the TV shows they watched and I didn't have my period yet and I didn't have a boyfriend. The more I was with them, surrounded by them, the more separate I felt, not just from them but from myself. And the girl

I spotted watching me under the tree that first day still watched me.

I found out her name was Juleen Presque. They called her the brain and said she was stranger than snake's feet. I'd see her sometimes watching me surrounded by a group of girls, casting spells, and it seemed as if she were waiting, wanting something. I wondered if she wanted me to cast a spell for her, but she always stood apart, and when I tried to go up and speak to her, she walked away.

I didn't like her watching me like the old wig heads. Every time I saw her I got scared, and I felt this cold spot harden in the center of my chest. Any joy left in playing the love magician game died whenever she was around. Then later, toward the end of winter, the joy died altogether. I had replaced it with fear. That dark fear-shadow that had been with me for so long no longer hovered over and around me but had moved inside me, had taken over my whole insides so that I feared everything—the dark cracks in the sidewalk and tree branches broken off and lying dead on the ground. I was afraid of thunder and lightning and steep stairwells. I was afraid of choking on my food. Most of all, I was afraid that there was someone pushing me, or drawing me forward to someplace I didn't want to go, someplace dangerous, and every day I played the love magician game, every time someone fell for my tricks, it brought me closer to the edge of that dangerous place. Juleen Presque knew this. She was waiting for me to fall off that edge.

Then in the spring, Uncle Toole moved out on us, exactly one week before my fourteenth birthday. The last few days he had been with us, the house was quiet. They had stopped fighting. He and Aunt Casey had agreed that they had drifted apart. It was best they went on their own separate journeys, followed their own bliss. That's what Aunt Casey told me. Uncle Toole said, "Casey's just plain no fun anymore. My philosophy is you only go around once in life so drink your beer first."

Aunt Casey told him he had to move all his junk—the broken furniture and appliances—out of the house. I had hidden the overflow of candle bottles under those stacks of furniture and had to wait until they went to bed to dig them all out again. I spent most of the night searching for them and taking them in bags out to the garage, and even then I wasn't sure I'd found them all.

The next afternoon when I came home from school the house was so empty, so quiet. The old clutter had been comforting, like the voice of a radio in an empty house. It held its own noises, its own busyness. I always had to work my way around it to get anywhere. It took concentration not to stub my toe on a protruding leg, or to find my way to the kitchen and dig up a clean dish. The house was bare, exposed, stripped naked. I started to shiver. I stood in the living room, staring down at the only thing left: three candle bottles. Three. Bad things always happen in threes. Uncle Toole had moved out. One down, two to go. I grabbed up the candle bottles and brought them to my room. I pulled out the ones I had stashed under my sofabed, set them up around me on the floor, and lit them. I was still shivering. I put on Dane's bathrobe, but it didn't help. I brought the candle bottles in closer, but I was still cold. I climbed into the bed and huddled under the covers, but I couldn't stop the shaking. My teeth were chattering. I felt cold from the inside out instead of the outside in. I stayed huddled in my blankets and watched the candles melt. I grew colder still.

Aunt Casey came home at night and called out to me. Her voice sounded far away. She came to my bedroom and knocked on my door.

"Can I come in?" She opened the door without waiting for an answer. She saw the candle bottles. "Hey, what's going on? What are you doing with all those candles?"

Then she saw me shivering in the bed.

"What—are you sick? I've never known you to get sick before."

She set her backpack on the floor and moving to the bed reached out her hand to touch my forehead. "You don't seem to have a fever. Maybe I should take your temperature."

"No. I'm okay."

"How 'bout I fix you some hot tea?"

"Okay."

Aunt Casey turned to leave. On her way out of the room she said, "I thought we lost all those bottles in the tornado."

She returned with the tea and some toast and I sat up. She set the tray on my lap, but I was shivering so much the tea was slopping out of the mug.

"I'll just move the tray onto the bed here, okay? I brought you some toast."

I nodded and reached for the mug. I had to concentrate hard to keep my hands from shaking the tea out again. I took a sip and I could feel the heat traveling in a thin stream down the center of my body. I kept drinking, but the heat wouldn't spread out to my arms or legs or feet. I took a bite of the toast.

"I always liked tea and toast when I was sick," Aunt Casey said, standing over me and watching me eat and drink.

The toast had mold on it. I could taste it. I drank down the rest of the tea and by the time I had finished it, the tea inside me had gone cold and I was still shivering.

"I can't eat the toast," I said. "Sorry."

"You want some more tea?"

"No, I just want to lie down."

"Okay, but I'm blowing out these candles. We don't want a fire. Did you notice the living room?"

"Yes." I huddled back down under the covers again.

"My voice echoes in it. The house hasn't been this clean since I was a kid."

I lifted my head. "You lived here when you were a kid?"

Aunt Casey nodded and picked up her backpack. "Yup. I've always lived here. Didn't you know that?"

"Mama—Sissy lived here?"

"This was our bedroom, sure. Didn't you know that?"

"No." I rolled over and faced the wall. I didn't want to know any more. I could feel myself getting close to that dangerous place again. I could almost peer over the edge. I didn't want to see what was there. I didn't want to find out any more. I was afraid to even think about Dane or Mama because I just knew if I did Aunt

Casey would leave, too. That's how it worked. That was the connection.

"Well, I'll check on you in the morning. Think you need a doctor or anything?"

"No," I mumbled from beneath the blankets. I felt so cold.

I know I slept some. I remembered dreaming about a warm yellow light. I could see it on the other side of a giant spider web. The web was blocking my way. I stood in the cold dark just inches from the warmth, too afraid to walk through the web.

When I woke up I was still shivering. Aunt Casey brought me some tea and some more moldy toast and sat on the edge of my bed. She watched me drink my tea. She stared at my face, studied it the same way she studied for her psychology exams, with the same intense expression. It was as if she were trying to read me, understand me. She opened her mouth a few times and I thought she would say something; I could tell there was something she felt she needed to say. And watching her, seeing her trying to find the right words, I felt I could almost will those words out of her mouth for her, I could almost guess at what they would be, and then I couldn't do it. Fear gripped my hands and shook the tea onto my lap. I dropped the mug onto the tray, and Aunt Casey jumped up and brushed at her own lap as if I had spilled some on her. Then she removed the tray and dabbed at my lap with the napkin she'd brought me. The mood had been broken. She said different words than the ones she had planned to say, safer words. She said she would come home early and if I didn't feel better she'd take me to see her doctor.

"Of course, it could just be psychosomatic. Know what that is? When it's all in your mind. Most illnesses are all in the mind, did you know that? Disease is just dis-ease. Without ease. Cool, huh?"

I shivered all day long. I couldn't get warm. I stayed facing the wall. The wig heads were behind me. Aunt Casey had let me keep them turned away. She said it was easier to get at the wigs that way anyway, but I still felt afraid of them. I was afraid if I turned one of them back around again, any one of them, they'd have someone's live face on them. Maybe Mrs. Beane's, the woman who came for her fitting and died two months later. Maybe the head her wig sat on would have her face. That's what I feared. They all had the faces of the person whose wigs they wore.

I tried not to think about them, or anyone. I counted to ten thousand over and over, but sometimes a thought would slip in if I let my mind relax too much. I'd get a glimpse of Gigi in her home in Tennessee. Home since Christmas, yet I hadn't seen her since the tornado. I hadn't seen Grandaddy Opal, either. I wouldn't think about that—six thousand and eighty-two—Miss Emmaline always answering the phone now—six thousand, four hundred, and thirty-one—Juleen Presque, the brain—eight thousand twenty-six—Dane melted—eight thousand forty-two—Gigi—don't think—I'm so cold—nine thousand and thirteen.

The doorbell rang. I lifted my head. Was it Aunt Casey? It rang again. Uncle Toole? I climbed out of the bed and hurried to the door, dragging the top blanket with me.

I opened the door and found Juleen Presque standing on the stoop in front of me.

I sucked in my breath and choked on the quick draw of air. "I'm sick, go away," I said, coughing, pressing against the door.

Juleen pushed it back and stepped inside. "I brought your homework." She held up a stack of books. "You're shivering. Why don't you get back in bed. I can talk to you there."

"No. No, I'm fine." I didn't want her seeing the wig heads or the sawed-off sofa I slept in. "Thanks for the books." I cleared my throat and clutched the blanket around my shoulders. "How did you get my homework? You're not in any of my classes."

"But I was in your English class last year," she said, peering into the empty living room.

"You were? I don't remember."

"That took guts coming in new the last month of school and messing with Mr. Pertnoy's head."

I shook my head. "I don't remember."

"Erasing your name, reading that crazy story with the pirouettes."

"Oh! Oh yeah. He gave me an incomplete." I wrapped my blanket around me tighter. I wished she'd leave the books and go away. "So thanks for the books then. I'll probably be back in school tomorrow."

"I've been watching you," she said, walking toward the kitchen.

I followed her. "I know."

She turned around to face me. "You're very interesting."

"Thanks." I looked away at the empty counters—no cannons or Confederate mugs, no ashtrays or old newspapers. I was so cold.

Juleen stepped closer to me. "You're a clever one."

"I don't know..."

"You're smart. You had the whole school believing in you, in your spells and dances and that story about descending from a long line of mediums and clairvoyants."

"But it's true. My grandmother's a medium."

"And now it's all backfired. Now everybody knows," Juleen said, ignoring me.

"Backfired? What's backfired? What does everybody know?" Why didn't she leave? I was freezing. Couldn't she see I was freezing?

"Melanie Brubaker came in today with her purple hair."

"Melanie?"

"You told her to dye her hair purple and do that stupid dance in front of Bob Eliott, remember?"

"Yes. Didn't it work? She must not have..."

"Her hair fell out! All day long, in patches all over her head. Bob Eliott told her she was a joke and should join the circus. Everyone was laughing at her because of you."

"She must have done something..."

Juleen stuck her face right up to mine. I could feel her heat, but it wasn't enough to warm me.

"You're a phony. Everyone knows it now. A fake! I knew it. I could have told them, but I let you set yourself up. Everyone gets caught eventually—every fake."

"Stop!" I backed away. "I'm not a fake. I'm real. I'm real!"

"My aunt Juleen used to contact the dead." Juleen stared down at the books in her hands. "I was named after her, after a fake. She was caught red-handed. I was there when it happened. I used to think she was wonderful." She paused, then looked up at me. "Now you got caught, everybody knows, and your grandmother will get caught, too."

I took another step back and found myself up against the kitchen wall. "No. She won't. She's real."

"How do you know?"

"She is. Stop it! I've seen her. I was her assistant. People have even seen their dead husbands and wives appear right in front of them."

Juleen nodded. "People see what they want to see."

"What does that mean? What do you want? Why are you here?"

"It's all illusions, magic tricks. People see what they want to see and don't see what they don't want to see. The whole school knows now. They know what you really are. They know you're a fake."

"Stop saying that!" I didn't want her pushing me, making me look at what I didn't want to see. "I'm sick. You'd better go now."

"It's dangerous what you're doing. People could get hurt worse than Melanie. Don't mess with magic."

"You need to go now." I let go of my blanket and took my schoolbooks from her.

"I brought you a book. See there on top. It's a book of poetry. Do you read poetry?"

"What?" This girl was crazy. I had to get rid of her.

"I read poetry. I write it, too. It helps."

I pushed Juleen toward the door. "Thanks for the book. Honest, I don't feel well. You have to go."

Juleen opened the door and paused, turning back to look at me. "You read the poems. They're true. They're the truest, realest thing I know. You need that, I think. You're like me. You need the truth."

Chapter 17

I WAS STILL SHIVERING, but I didn't put the covers back over me. My hands felt stiff, frozen. It was hard turning the pages in my miracle notebook where I had glued a miracle story to almost every page—a story from the newspaper, a *true* story. Newspapers had to print the truth. Miracles happen. I was a miracle. Gigi said so. A miracle! I'm real. Juleen doesn't know anything. Nobody does. Gigi knows. She knows about things like that. She's a medium. She's the world's greatest medium! I've seen her. I've seen her working. She didn't have to pretend because it was real. She made her clients happy. They got to speak with their loved ones. Some said they actually saw them—*People see what they want to see*. No! It was real. I believe it. I'm real.

She used incense and wore robes and saw auras. She could go into a trance—*People see what they want to see and don't see what they don't want to see*. No! She could contact the dead. She had Rasmus, her spirit guide—

How do you know?—It's all illusions, magic tricks. No! I slammed my miracle notebook shut. I remembered the day in Grandaddy Opal's room. He showed me a book, a science book, a book of facts. It said there were black holes and wormholes and that space and time could bend in on themselves in a black hole. It said it. It is the truth. It was all true. It had to be true. I climbed on my bed and faced the shelf of wig heads. "It's true. It's all true," I said to the heads. "You *can* contact the dead. Gigi can. Gigi does. She contacted Mama that night. Mama told us Dane melted. No—Mama told us Dane was gone, and—and Gigi said he melted. But I saw it. He was gone. He did melt. See? See, it's true. It's all real. And I created love potions. They were real. They worked. It was real. I'm real!"

The wig heads just stayed there lined up on the shelves, the backs of their heads to me. They didn't believe me. I knew they didn't. I jumped off the bed. "I'll prove it. I'll show you—stupid wig heads!"

I ran barefoot out to the garage. I had to make several trips to get all the candle bottles. I pulled them out of the bags and set them up all over the room, leaving a space in the center for me. I lit the candles and stood among them in Dane's bathrobe and waited to melt.

"Come on, melt!"

I waited. I didn't even feel warm. How was I going to melt if I didn't get warm? I moved the candle bottles in closer together, closer to me. The wig heads were waiting. Everyone was. The kids at school, Gigi, Grandaddy Opal, Aunt Casey. They were waiting for me to prove myself, prove I was real.

I bent my knees so that the bottom of Dane's bathrobe hovered just above the flames of the bottles surrounding me. I waited. Yes, I was getting warmer. I closed my eyes and bent my knees just a little bit further.

Part II

*"The Truth must dazzle gradually
or every man be blind."*

—EMILY DICKINSON

Part II

"The Truth must dazzle gradually
or every man be blind."
—Emily Dickinson

Chapter 18

I DON'T REMEMBER much about my stay in the hospital, not those early days, at least. I don't remember how I got there. All I remember is sitting in a silver tub of water with my legs floating up at me like a couple of dead fish. I felt like a fish. I remember that, thinking I was a slice of haddock or cod. Gigi used to cook a lot of fish, white slabs of it on a platter with their shiny pink and silver backs. She would dredge each slab through her special egg and flour mixtures and fry them up crisp the way Dane liked it. My legs were frying. That's what it felt like. As if every day someone were dropping them into the deep fat and frying them up crisp. The doctor said I had second- and third-degree burns. I remember nodding when he said it. I remember sitting in that silver tub, staring down at my legs and thinking, *Yes, my legs are all burned up,* but I couldn't remember how they got that way, what had happened.

The nurses didn't like me to see the burns. They said I was already too traumatized and it was affecting the rate of healing. They wanted me to scream out in pain, but I didn't scream.

I learned that bits of rayon material had burned into some of the deeper wounds. The doctors rolled me into surgery to remove those bits and apply skin grafts. Then they put goop and dressings on my legs, and bulky pressure bandages on the grafts, and strung my legs up in the air so they would heal.

Gigi came to see me after my skin-grafting surgery. I pretended to be asleep. She took charge. She told the nurses what to do, ordering more fluids and painkillers even while I slept. She asked the doctors when I'd be able to leave and told them I could leave sooner. She had a place she could take me for healing. I'd heal faster with her, she said.

Aunt Casey came a lot, three times a day. I'd never seen her so often. She'd stare down at me with her red and swollen eyes, searching my eyes, my face, for some kind of answer. She'd talk to me, her voice tight, constricted. She asked how I was doing, if I needed anything. She told me I could scream if the pain got to be too much. It would be all right to scream, she said, just like the nurses, but I didn't scream. I didn't speak. I don't know why. I just lost the desire. I didn't speak to anyone.

They had a TV in my room. I had to share it with the patient in the bed next to me, a girl who had been thrown through the windshield of her car. She didn't watch TV. She always had too many people around her bed, talking with her, laughing.

The nurses didn't know that I had never seen a whole television show. They warned me that most of the shows were already in reruns for the season, but it was all new to me.

Miss Emmaline came once when Aunt Casey was in the room and said in a voice the whole floor could hear that Grandaddy Opal couldn't come because he was feeling a little under the weather himself. She said for me not to worry, that he would be better real soon and he couldn't wait to see his girl. Then she and Aunt Casey went out into the hallway to whisper, but Miss Emmaline wasn't good at whispering.

I heard her say that Grandaddy Opal was back in the hospital—third time in four months. She said they thought the bypass surgery had gone well but he wasn't recovering the way he should have. Then Aunt Casey spoke and I didn't hear what she said, but I understood anyway. Needing people too much just drove them away. Loving someone did something to their hearts. My need for Grandaddy Opal was too much and it gave him a heart attack. I was killing him. I drifted off to sleep and Miss Emmaline was gone when I woke up. I remembered what she had said about Grandaddy Opal, and I decided I wouldn't need him anymore. I couldn't think about him anymore.

I remember Uncle Toole coming to see me and he didn't know what to do besides stand there and change the channels on the television.

I started getting better. The nurses removed the pressure bandages. The oozing had stopped and they changed my dressings on the milder burns less frequently. I was down to taking painkillers only twice a day. I thought I'd be leaving soon.

Then a man came to see me. He was tall. He had

to duck to walk through the door. His legs were so long they didn't look as if they had been attached to his body correctly; his feet turned in slightly when he walked and his joints looked loose, as if he could stick his foot behind his head if he wanted to. He had on jeans with a shirt and tie and wore running shoes. He loped over to my bed and took my hand and shook it.

"Hi, Miracle, I'm Dr. DeAngelis. Mind if I sit down?"

He leaned forward over me, waiting for an answer. I stared at his hands. They were large and wide and hairy. He wore a wedding band.

"Yes, I heard you're not speaking. I don't know if you mind if I sit down or not, so since I want to stay, I'll have a seat."

He pulled up a chair, sat down, and propped his long feet up on the end of my bed.

"I know your aunt Casey. I lectured at the university last month. She was there. Very intelligent. Very nice."

He paused and studied me a few seconds. He was watching my hands. I tucked them under the covers.

"I saw pictures of your legs. They're healing quite nicely, but there's a lot of scarring, isn't there? Maybe down the road a little you can have a plastic surgeon help you with those scars." He took his feet off the bed and leaned forward so his head was near my shoulder. "I'm a doctor of scars, too, Miracle, only they're the kind of scars you can't see. They're inside you. I'm going to help you, if you'll let me. You see those wounds you have inside, they haven't healed quite as nicely as your legs.". He sat back in his seat, and I stared at the cup of water on the tray beside my bed.

"In a couple of days you're going to be transferred to another building called The Cedars, although I don't know why, there are no cedar trees. But I think you'll like it lots better. You don't have to stay in bed all day. You'll have things to do. You'll take classes and catch up on your schoolwork, and there'll be group therapy sessions where you'll be with other teens with similar problems . . ."

I looked up.

"Oh, you don't think anyone else has problems like yours. Well, that's what's so nice about group. You discover you're not alone. There are people out there who have the same feelings you do. You'll get to share your feelings. Maybe what you have to share will help somebody else. Maybe you'll hear things that will help you and those scars will start to melt away."

He paused again, letting his information sink in. His voice was soft for a man. Not like a woman's, just soft, as if he didn't want to disturb anyone. And he had an accent. He was from New York or New Jersey. My dance teacher, Susan, was from New York.

He touched my shoulder, cupped it in his big hand. "You'll visit with me several times a week as well. I'm looking forward to getting to know you better, Miracle. We'll talk, maybe play some games, draw some pictures, that sort of thing. And I'll have some sessions with your aunt and perhaps some of your other family members."

I started to shiver.

Dr. DeAngelis squeezed my shoulder. "It'll be all

right, Miracle. No surprises. I'm here today so you'll know what's going to happen. It may be scary, even painful at times, tearing through all that old scar tissue, I won't kid you, but I and the staff, we're all there for you. We're there to help you."

He stood up and patted my head. I pulled away. "I'll see you in a few days. If you have any questions or want to talk to me before then you just let them know and I'll come over as soon as I can."

I watched him walk away, ducking back through the door. I stopped shivering when I heard the sound of his running shoes at the far end of the hall.

Chapter 19

Aunt Casey stood by my bed and picked at her fingernail polish the next time she came to see me. Her eyes were clear, but they kept moving while she talked to me, glancing at the windows, the walls, my legs, the floor, anything but me. She said she wanted to explain about seeing Dr. DeAngelis, about staying in the hospital.

"I know it's ... weird ... you know, talking to a stranger and all. I mean, no one in the family's ever done that—talked about problems with a stranger, I don't think. We don't even talk to each other ... really ... so talking with a stranger ... I know, it's weird." Aunt Casey stopped picking at her nail polish and rubbed her hands up and down her arms as if she were cold.

"At work, clients talk to me all the time—you know? They tell me all kinds of personal stuff while I'm doing their hair, even if it's their first time in. But it's weird being on the other side, being the one who's doing the

talking, taking someone else's advice. But Miracle"—
Aunt Casey glanced at my shoulders—"this family's got
too many secrets. We need help sorting it all out, the
secrets, and ... and problems. In my textbooks there are
all these case studies, I mean really strange cases, like
a man who can't find his head and this lady who thinks
she's a circus horse, and you know, they get cured! They
go home and lead normal healthy lives. All these wacko
cases, so just think how easy it'll be for us. So ... so, it's
not a bad thing. I mean, you didn't do anything bad.
It's not a punishment or anything. I'm not ... I'm just
wanting to help you." Aunt Casey frowned, her gaze
settling on my bedcovers. "It's the right thing to do."
She nodded. "It's the right thing to do."

THE NEXT DAY was moving day. I was going to another
wing of the hospital, a locked wing they called the
yellow unit. Aunt Casey said she'd go with me and
planned to come by at two-thirty in the afternoon. At
two-fifteen, Gigi showed up with a hospital attendant
who was holding the back of an empty wheelchair.

Gigi bustled into the room. "Come on," she said,
gesturing to the chair. "Hop in, it's time to go."

"But what about Aunt Casey, wasn't she ..."

Gigi waved her hand. "That's all changed. Now
hop in the chair, you've got to leave here riding one of
these so you don't fall and sue the hospital. Come on.
Come on."

I shuffled to the chair, with Gigi beckoning to me
the whole time, urging me to hurry.

"Good, good," she said when I was finally in the seat
and the orderly was rolling me out the door. We rode

the elevator to the main level and then they wheeled me down the corridor to the exit. That's when we ran into Aunt Casey.

"Where are you going?" Aunt Casey said, blocking the exit, her hands on her hips.

Gigi stepped in front of my chair so that I was looking at the back of her robe. "We're going home, what do you think? Now get out of the way."

"She's not going home," Aunt Casey said. "It's already been arranged."

"Well, unarrange it. How can you think of locking Miracle up in a cage and letting her be electrocuted?"

"Gigi!" Aunt Casey leaned sideways beyond Gigi's body and said to me, "It's not like that at all." Then to Gigi she said, "Stop trying to scare her. She needs help. We *all* do."

"That's right, and I can cure her in two days," Gigi said, stepping around to the back of my chair and bumping the orderly out of the way so she could hold the chair herself. "She doesn't need some prying, nosy doctor getting into our business. All those silly questions he asked me. It's not his business, and I told him so."

"Ah! That's what it is." Aunt Casey nodded. "You're afraid she'll learn the truth. You're afraid . . ."

Gigi raised her voice. "You've never liked this family. Never! You never liked Miracle. You only stick around because you feel guilty. It's guilt. It's all your fault. I should think you wouldn't get within a hundred miles of a shrink. You want Miracle to learn the truth? I can tell her the truth."

I didn't know what they were talking about. They

stood leaning over the chair, face-to-face, arguing with each other as if I weren't even there. They didn't even notice that the man had left. I saw him through the gap between Gigi's sleeve and Aunt Casey's arm. Both of them had their weight on the chair, claiming it for themselves. The man was making a phone call. I closed my eyes and listened to the words pelting my ears, making my head ache.

Gigi had accused Aunt Casey of not being able to afford to keep me in the hospital even one more day. She said that she and Eugene weren't going to pay for it and that was that, so Casey should let go of the chair. Aunt Casey stood up and puffed up her chest, reminding Gigi that she *owned* Hair Etcetera, and that she had all kinds of insurance on the salon and the stylists who worked there.

"When it came time to renew the health insurance last year, I simply put Miracle on my policy," she said. "If it's one thing I know, I've always had a good head for business. So now *you* get out of the way."

"Insurance! What good is that?"

"It'll at least cover a few more weeks in the hospital," Aunt Casey said, yanking on the chair.

"And what will a few weeks buy her? Half a cure?" Gigi yanked back.

"No, half a chance, which is more than she ever got with any of us. Now you let go!"

"I won't! You let go."

The two of them were pushing and shoving the chair back and forth between them when Dr. DeAngelis showed up.

"It looks as if we have a problem," he said, coming up behind me and Gigi.

Gigi let go of the chair and fled without saying another word. She was just a flash of purple sweeping through the exit. Aunt Casey stared after her and didn't move to take my chair.

Dr. DeAngelis cleared his throat. "Well, then, shall we go?" He turned my chair around and Aunt Casey, nodding, still speechless, came around to the side of my chair, and the three of us traveled down the hallway to the locked doors of the yellow unit.

Chapter 20

THE YELLOW UNIT. Yellow. Gigi said a yellow aura
means the person values his mind the most and
pursues the highest intellectual matters. The walls
of the yellow unit were blue. The floors were tan
linoleum, except in Dr. DeAngelis's office. He had a
gray carpet and white walls and black furniture, except for the couch. I couldn't figure out what color the
couch was.

They had me take some tests. I sat alone in a room
with computer-printed tests and a pencil. The tests
were different from the ones we took in school. These
tests had statements like: I think I am attractive—
A. All of the time. B. Some of the time. C. Never. Or,
I enjoy being with my friends—A. All of the time.
B. Some of the time. C. Never.

I left the answers blank.

They took me to the dayroom and told me for the
first two days I had to sleep there on the couch in front
of the night staff and then, if I behaved myself, I would

be given a real room. I didn't know what they meant. Behaved myself in what way?

The dayroom had couches and chairs that looked like Uncle Toole had donated them from his collection. Two large round tables stood in the middle and there was a Ping-Pong table to one side and the glassed-in nurses' station on the other. Red tape ran along the floor between the second table and the Ping-Pong table. I was told that for the first two days I couldn't step over the red line. This was very important. Everyone who came up to me—counselors, day nurses, Dr. DeAngelis—told me I could not step over the red tape. If I did, I'd have to spend another night in the dayroom. If I did, I'd lose points.

They had a point system. I lost twenty-five points for erasing my name off the blackboard on the wall across from the nurses' station. I lost 150 points the first day for erasing my name six times. They didn't put it up again. The blackboard had said, Miracle McCloy: Restricted.

They gave us points for making our beds and points for taking a shower. We got points for attending classes and group and for participating in group. We got points for dressing in the morning and behaving ourselves and for listening to the counselors. Six hundred points put you at level four. Five hundred at level three, four hundred at level two, and three hundred and below at level one. Level ones couldn't walk the grounds, have visitors, fix snacks in the kitchen, watch television, or go to the cafeteria to eat. My meals were brought to me, and I ate in the dayroom alone because I was the only level one.

The patients in the yellow unit called it the suicide ward or the psycho ward. There were seven of us in all. Gigi said seven is a miraculous number, full of meaning. One is unity, plus six is perfection. Seven also represents the life of the body: spirit, flesh, humor, and bone, and the life of the soul: passion, desire, reason. Seven was the perfect number.

I had my first real session with Dr. DeAngelis my second day on the yellow unit. Kyla, the day staffer, came and got me. I was in the dayroom, looking out the big window with the painted white grille over it. Someone told me they put the grilles on all the windows to keep the patients from punching out the glass. I was watching Aunt Casey and Uncle Toole walking away from the yellow unit. Both of them were talking. I could see their mouths moving at the same time, and I wondered if both of them were talking, who was listening?

"Come on, sugar, Dr. DeAngelis is waiting for you," Kyla said, taking my hand and pulling me away from the window.

People touched me all the time on the yellow unit. When Kyla introduced me to the group on the first day, she stood next to me and rubbed my back. Mike, the group therapist, touched my arm and asked me to join in the group discussion anytime I felt like it. Leah, one of the other patients, slapped the back of my head because I didn't answer her questions. She wanted to know why I was walking like Frankenstein, what was under the bandages. She lost one hundred points and kitchen privileges for hitting me.

I wasn't used to being touched, but I liked it. Every time someone touched me I imagined them placing a new piece of skin on me, as if they were giving me back a lost piece of myself.

Dr. DeAngelis was sitting at his desk taking notes when Kyla showed me into the room. He jumped up from his desk and smiled and pumped both my hands as if we were old friends. He told me to take a seat anywhere I liked, and Kyla left us alone.

I turned to the right three times and then to the left. I chose the black chair with the shiny silver legs in the far corner of the room, circled it three times, and sat down.

Dr. DeAngelis pulled his chair out from behind his desk and rolled it to the center of the room before sitting. It was no fair that his chair had wheels when the others didn't.

"Casey explained to me about the circling," he said. "She was here just before you. Your grandmother, Gigi, is a firm believer in the supernatural, isn't she?"

I looked past him at the poster he had above his desk. It was of a runner running down a lonely road toward the mountains and the sun. Written above the runner it said THE MIND SET FREE.

Dr. DeAngelis twisted around with his chair to look at the poster. "Like it? It's my favorite." He twisted back to me. "Do you run? I do. I love to run.

"No, you dance, don't you? Let's see..." He wheeled himself backward toward his desk and reached for his notes. Then he rolled forward again, a little closer to me this time, and flipped through his yellow notepad.

"Yes, Emmaline Wilson said you were a dancer, quite good, too."

171

He looked at me. "You look surprised. Let's see what else do I know about you?" He flipped back through his notes.

I didn't like it. I didn't like him having me there on his paper. I jumped up from my chair and ran for the door.

He raised his voice. "Nothing. Almost nothing. Your relatives know surprisingly little about you, Miracle."

I waited with my hand on the doorknob. "They couldn't tell me what your interests were, who your friends are, what your favorite foods are, your favorite color—well, you always wear purple, don't you? But that's at your grandmother's request, is that right?"

He waited as if I were going to answer him.

"Come sit down, Miracle."

It was a command not a request. His voice wasn't so soft. His gaze followed me back to my chair.

"Very good. I'm wondering why no one can give me much information on you. They tell me you lived with your grandmother. And then you moved in with your grandfather. So then you lived with your grandmother and grandfather? And they are divorced."

He returned to his notes. "Then there was a tornado and your grandfather had a heart attack—a warning, I believe Miss Wilson called it. Two days later he had a more serious attack, it almost killed him." I scratched at my arm. I wouldn't think about Grandaddy Opal, how I almost killed him.

He looked up at me. "Miss Wilson says you and he were quite close. He talks about you all the time. You must have been quite upset by the attacks." He waited. "Miracle, your arm's bleeding." He grabbed a tissue

172

from the box on his desk and handed it to me. I wrapped it around my arm without looking at it, without thinking about Grandaddy. I rubbed my nose and looked away.

He went back to the notes. "Then you went to live with your aunt and uncle. Back to Alabama. Whew!" He looked at me again. "That's quite a lot of moving. It's hard, isn't it? Leaving what you're used to—your friends, your home, and in your case, your family."

He rolled his chair toward me. I pushed mine back, but there was nowhere to go so the front legs just lifted off the floor. Dr. DeAngelis rolled all the way up to me and took my hands in his.

"I'm sorry for your loss, Miracle." He looked directly into my eyes, and I turned away and looked at the blank wall. He reached up and took my chin and pulled my face forward again.

"When we communicate in this room, we look at each other, eye to eye. That's one of my rules, Miracle."

He held my face, but I kept my eyes down. I couldn't look at him.

"Miracle, I think you've gotten a bum deal. I think things have been pretty rotten for you at times. It makes me angry. Miracle, I'm very angry."

I looked at him, right in the eyes, and there was a face looking back at me—a tiny, angry face staring out at me from the center of his eyes.

Chapter 21

EVERYONE THOUGHT I had set myself on fire. I wasn't sure, I couldn't remember. Leah had cut her wrist. She had a large white bandage wrapped around it, but she liked to pull it away and look at the slits. She showed them to me and asked to see my legs. I wouldn't show her. I still had to have goop smeared on them twice a day, and new dressings put on. I wore my purple pants to keep them covered up. They still hurt. Sometimes at night I'd wake up with them on fire all over again, that's what it felt like. I thought maybe because I didn't feel it the first time, when it happened, I was going to have to feel the pain every day for the rest of my life.

Everyone there liked to talk about what they had done to themselves. They would remind each other over and over, show their scars, tell their story—horror stories. I knew I wasn't in the right place.

In group, Mike, the counselor, asked for suggestions

for ways of handling our anger and depression, ways of dealing with disappointment. Leah said the best way was to cut yourself. Jon said it was to OD on drugs. Then the others started in, and Kyla had to clap her hands and tell everyone to stop acting out.

They liked to act crazy in group, too, say crazy things like "I'm a cat," and then crawl around on all fours and lick people's legs. They did it on purpose, a show for the counselors.

The girls all liked Mike. He looked like a tennis player. He wore pink shirts and white tennis shorts and had a tennis tan.

Mike asked me for a suggestion, and when I didn't answer, Leah shouted, "Talk!" Then they all started chanting, "Talk, talk, talk, talk!" Kyla had to clap several times and threaten them with losing points before they would hush up.

After two days in the yellow unit, they gave me a bedroom. I shared it with Deborah. She was eighteen years old, pretty, with big bright blue eyes and dark eyelashes, and she was very fat. She liked to cuddle with people, especially Kyla. She had taken sleeping pills because her boyfriend had dumped her. She had engraved his name on her arm. She showed it to me. It was brown. Roy, carved in brown. It looked like a little child wrote it. She said she did it with the metal clip broken off her father's Parker Brothers pen. "My father made me get a tetanus shot for it," she said, holding it up for me to see and then bringing her arm back in close to her and staring at it a long time, as if she had never seen it before.

175

She told me Roy left her for someone who didn't do things like scratch her boyfriend's name in her arm. She said he was afraid of the commitment a Roy scar demanded.

I couldn't have any visitors for two weeks. I didn' mind. I didn't know who would come visit me any way—maybe Uncle Toole. They had a television set i the TV room and it was on all day. He could sit with me and change the channels.

Anytime I didn't have to be in class, or in group, o sitting with Dr. DeAngelis, or eating, I watched tele vision. Everyone fought over which programs to watch but I didn't care what I watched: Every bit of it fasci nated me—the way kids talked to their parents and the way parents talked to each other. The people on TV always had something funny to say, or something smart or they were goofy and weird but people talked to them anyway.

Kyla always knew where to find me when it was time to go see Dr. DeAngelis. She called me a couch potato I had never heard of a couch potato before, but it made me think of the potato chips I found under the cushion of my bed in Aunt Casey's wig room. I slept with them under me a long time and then one night, back when I was just starting to fear the dark, I ate them.

Kyla always took my hand when we walked down the hall to Dr. DeAngelis's office. I think she was afraid I would fall if I walked on my own.

One time when I went to see Dr. DeAngelis, he had the stack of schoolbooks Juleen Presque had dropped off at the house sitting on his desk.

"Your aunt Casey brought these with her today," he

said when he saw that I had noticed them. "You can take them with you when you leave."

I took my usual seat and Dr. DeAngelis stood up and said, "No, Miracle, I'd like you to take my seat today and I'll sit in yours." We traded chairs. I sat down behind his desk. His notes were cleared away. I saw a picture of a woman with three teenaged children—two boys, one girl. The tallest boy looked like Dr. DeAngelis and the other two looked like the woman. They were all huddled together as if they were cold. The wind was blowing their hair back from their faces. I turned the picture face down on the desk.

"Is there something there that interests you, Miracle?" Dr. DeAngelis asked.

He surprised me. I had forgotten he was there. I pushed myself away from his desk and tried to wheel myself toward the door, but my legs hurt too much. I got up out of the chair and pushed it up against the door. I was about to sit back down when Dr. DeAngelis spoke.

"That paper on the desk is for you. I'd like you to draw a picture for me today. Would you roll the chair back to the desk, please?"

I didn't want to draw. In art class people made fun of my drawings. They said I drew like a little kid. One art teacher wanted to hold a conference with Gigi and the school psychologist. They sent a note home to Gigi. Gigi wrote back that she'd look into it, and that was the end of that.

"Miracle, take the chair back to my desk and sit down, please."

I did as he told me and found the large white sheet

of paper there on the desk. There were colored pencils off to the side, next to my schoolbooks.

"This is not for a grade, Miracle. I don't even care how good you are." Dr. DeAngelis shifted in his chair, sitting up straighter.

"This is an opportunity for you to express yourself. We don't always need to talk to express ourselves, do we? We can use gestures, facial expressions. We can write or draw or build things. Today, I'd like you to draw a picture of me sitting in this chair, just as I am now."

I hesitated.

"It's all right."

I picked out the purple pencil. He needed to be purple. His aura was black. I looked up at him sitting in his chair, tucked in the corner.

He's scared, that's why. That's why he's way back there. There's so much danger. He must wear his purple for protection. And his bathrobe. His bathrobe will protect me. And I'll draw my aura, my black aura, and my legs are on fire, I have to show my legs are on fire.

I looked up from my drawing.

"Are you through?" Dr. DeAngelis stood up and stretched. His fists touched the ceiling. He came over to the desk and lifted my drawing to examine it.

What did I draw? I couldn't remember. He wouldn't like it. He'd laugh. I watched him, waiting for his eyes to crinkle up, for his smirk.

"Thank you, Miracle," he said, and his face was serious. "This is just what I wanted. May I keep it?"

178

I looked away at my schoolbooks with the book of poems, Juleen's book, lying on top.

"Eye contact, please."

I lifted my head.

"Very good. I'd like to keep your drawing. Is that all right with you?"

I didn't know. I couldn't remember what I had drawn. He told me to draw him sitting in the chair, but did I? He seemed pleased. I must have done it right.

"Miracle." Dr. DeAngelis leaned forward, setting his palms on his desk. I could smell his aftershave lotion. Uncle Toole wore Brut aftershave. This smelled different, maybe it was soap. "Miracle, if you don't communicate your wishes to me, then I get to choose what I wish. You are giving me the power to choose. You're giving me your power, a power you have a right to own yourself. You understand?"

I took a deep breath of his clean smell, and he stood back up and said the session was over. He reminded me to take my books with me on the way out.

I took the books back to my room and set them on my bed. I was about to return to the TV room when I remembered the poetry book Juleen had left me. I picked it up and opened it, and saw by the dates in the introduction that the author of the poems, Emily Dickinson, was dead. A slip of paper was poking out of the book, marking a page. I opened it to the marker. There was the shortest little poem on the page. I read it. I read it again, and I could hear Juleen's voice saying, "You read the poems. They're true. They're the truest, realest thing I know."

I read the first lines again: "I'm Nobody! Who are you? Are you—Nobody—Too? Then there's a pair of us? Don't tell! they'd advertise—you know!"

I tossed the book down and cried out. I didn't know if it was in shock, or pain, or joy, or fear. I just cried out. For the first time in my life I had recognized my reflection.

Chapter 22

"S HE'S CRACKING UP! Get a sedative! Get a sedative!"
Leah had run into the room and was trying to pull
me up off the floor. Deborah and Kyla came in behind
her, and Kyla told her to hush, everything would be just
fine.

Kyla got down on the floor and pulled me to her.
I didn't want to be held. I didn't want to be touched.
I fought her. I cried and yelled and pushed her
away.

Joe, another nurse, pushed through the group standing in the doorway and grabbed me up off the floor and
held me, his arm coming down from behind and
crossing my chest. He and Kyla kept saying, "It's okay.
It's all right." I kept fighting and crying.

Leah said, "Get her a sedative. Why don't you get
her a sedative? She's cracked, look at her, she's cracked.
Put her in the seclusion room. How come you don't put
her in the seclusion room?"

Kyla left me with Joe and clapped her hands. She told everyone to get to the dayroom. Anyone not there in five seconds would lose twenty points.

Then I heard Dr. DeAngelis's voice behind me repeating what Kyla had said, and then, "It's all right, Joe. I'll take her back with me."

Joe released me and left. The room was quiet except for my own noise. I was still crying and yelling and fighting with the air, flinging my arms out. I don't remember what I said, if I even used real words—I don't remember.

I kept my back to Dr. DeAngelis. I fought my way to the corner of the room and stopped. I pressed my head against the wall. I stopped shouting and just cried. I cried a long time, and it was so quiet behind me I wasn't sure if Dr. DeAngelis had left or if he was still with me. I could hear the group in the dayroom. I could hear Leah talking about the time she cracked. The tears stopped running down my face. I stood in the corner sniffling, listening for Dr. DeAngelis. I couldn't hear him. I turned around to look for him, and he was there.

"Hello, Miracle. Yes, I'm here."

"Go away!" I turned back to the wall.

"Is that what you really want?"

"Yes!"

"All right. I'll have to take you out to the nurses' station. You need to be watched. Miracle? You must go out to the nurses' station for now."

I turned around. "Okay then, I'll go with you."

"Good, I'd like that."

We walked back down the hallway to his office. I could hear Mike asking the group, "How are we feeling when we cry?"

Dr. DeAngelis told me to sit in the chair near his desk. He rolled his chair in front of it and sat down. He handed me a tissue from the tissue box on his desk and I blew my nose. Then we sat in silence for a few minutes. I played with the edges of my tissue. He folded his hands in his lap.

"You were very upset back there, weren't you? Can you tell me about it? You were angry, weren't you? What else?"

"Nothing."

"Eye contact, please."

I lifted my head and said louder, in his face, "Nothing! Nobody! I'm nobody, who are you?"

Dr. DeAngelis smiled and his eyes crinkled into smiling slits. "Emily Dickinson's poem, right?"

"No. It's mine."

"You can relate to it."

"Yes."

"Eye contact, please."

"Yes! Yes, it's me. It's nobody. It's me."

"And that makes you feel—what?"

"Nothing."

"Empty?"

"Yes, nothing. I don't feel anything. I didn't even feel my legs."

"When? Miracle, look at me. When?"

"The fire. I didn't feel it." I tore at my tissue. I needed to throw it away, it was wet.

Dr. DeAngelis handed me two more tissues. "You didn't feel it burn your legs?"

"No! I'm nobody. I feel nothing." I wrapped my soggy tissue in one of the others and let it fall to the floor. I scrunched the other one up in my hand.

Dr. DeAngelis leaned forward, resting his elbows on his knees. His toes were pointing in toward each other.

"Miracle, you must have felt something. Something led you to set yourself on fire—anger or hurt or fear or sadness—something."

"No. I don't remember. I don't know."

"We don't always know what we're feeling until we act it out by crying or shouting, or by hurting ourselves. I'd like to try to help you learn to identify your feelings."

"I'm nobody, who are you?"

"What do you think you were feeling in your room a few minutes ago? What made you cry out? I heard you all the way down here. That must have been an awfully strong feeling to release such a cry."

"Nothing."

"Eye contact, Miracle."

I lifted my head but didn't repeat myself.

Dr. DeAngelis sat back and loosened his tie. His tie was navy blue with tiny red words written in slanted lines all the way down. I thought they were thin red stripes at first but up close I could see that it said "RunRunRunRun."

"What feelings might a person have when they're crying, Miracle?"

It was the same question I had heard Mike ask the group. I wished I'd listened to their answers. I shrugged.

"Are they happy, do you think?"

I shrugged again. "Sometimes, maybe."

"Okay. What else?"

"Sad?"

He nodded. "Yes, good. Name three more."

Bad things happen in threes. "I don't know three," I said.

"Tell me what you know. What do you think you felt back in your room?"

"I don't know." I tore my new tissue. I pulled a hole in the center, then scrunched it back up. "Sad maybe and—and scared."

"Ah, scared." Dr. DeAngelis nodded. "What scared you?"

"Everything—me—everything scares me."

"Can you give me examples? What are some things that scare you?"

I twisted away, grabbing on to the back of my chair.

"Eye contact, please."

I shook my head. "No, I can't."

"You're afraid of looking at me? What do you think you might see? Miracle?"

"I'm afraid of the dark. I'm afraid to see."

"You're afraid of something in the dark? Of seeing something in the dark?"

I nodded.

Dr. DeAngelis's soft voice got softer, a whisper. "What's there in the dark? I'm with you, Miracle, right here. What do you see in the dark?"

I turned back around. I had my eyes closed. "Nothing. I don't want to see." I shook my head. I shook it and shook it. "I don't want to see. I don't want to see. I don't want to see."

Chapter 23

THE NURSE GAVE ME an extra pill to take when I came back from seeing Dr. DeAngelis. Everyone called them my meds. "Did she give you your meds?" It seemed all the patients were on meds. When they weren't comparing horror stories, they were comparing meds. "What do they have you on? Stelazine? Mellaril?" I didn't talk to any of the other patients except Deborah. I didn't talk in group.

The pill made me sleepy. They let me go to bed early and skip dinner. It was my first time sleeping through the night since I moved in with Aunt Casey. I hadn't slept at all during the night since I had been on the yellow unit. I took catnaps during the day, in front of the TV. At night I was awake. I listened to Deborah's light snore, almost a whistle. I stared out at the shadows. I watched them to make sure they didn't move, the ones in the corner and against the wall across from me, and stretching out from the ceiling light. I didn't want them inching up closer. I watched them all night except when the nurses came around for checks. I'd hear the night nurse open our door and I'd shut my eyes until her check was over.

I didn't want them to give me that sleeping pill again. That's just what the shadows were waiting for—me to sleep. I was lucky once, but I didn't trust my luck. I didn't trust the shadows.

AUNT CASEY came to see me—my first visitor. I had earned enough points to walk the grounds with her. She carried her backpack on her shoulder, and I noticed she could walk better in her sandals. She had cut her hair, too. It was short and slicked back with some kind of goop. It reminded me of the goop the nurses put on my legs.

The grounds were nice, lots of fresh-cut lawn that smelled like watermelon, and pine trees that stood in clusters everywhere, and azaleas already past blooming, and magnolias that hadn't blossomed yet.

There was a path that led to some picnic tables. Aunt Casey and I followed the path out to the tables and sat down at one under the pine trees. She flopped her backpack on the table and unzipped it.

"You know," she said, "I don't even know what kind of sandwiches you like. You lived with us a year, almost exactly a year, and I don't even remember ever fixing you anything. I didn't, did I? Miracle?"

I had been staring into the sun. I looked at Aunt Casey and she looked hazy; a dark fuzzy aura surrounded her. I blinked, trying to blink the sun out of my eyes so I could see her better.

"Anyway, I brought you three choices—egg salad,

187

tuna, or peanut butter and jelly—which do you want?"

I reached for the egg salad.

She pulled two cans of root beer out of her pack and set one down in front of me. I noticed she'd cut her fingernails short, no nail polish. The nails looked yellow. Yellow, the color of intellectual pursuits.

"The doctor said you are talking now. I guess you're too angry to talk to me." Aunt Casey watched me a few seconds, then took the tuna sandwich and unwrapped it. "I don't blame you. Here I am taking all these psychology courses and there you were right under my nose and I didn't see it, or maybe I didn't want to see it." Aunt Casey took a bite of her sandwich and I took a bite of mine. It tasted good. The best thing they served in the cafeteria was the Jell-O, until it got several days old and wouldn't glide down the throat anymore. They served Jell-O every day—red Jell-O, the color of fire and rage.

"I've been carrying around a sh—a bucket load of anger myself, you know," Aunt Casey said. "I've been running away from it, burying it. Doing just what every one of my textbooks says is the worst thing we can do, and there I was reading all that and nodding and taking notes and not even knowing it was just what I was doing." She took another bite and stared at the sky. It was the bluest blue, a spiritual blue, Gigi would say. Uncle Toole would call it a sweet Alabama blue.

"That Toole and all his messing around," Aunt Casey said, swallowing her bite. "I could have shot him. Really, I could have. I truly considered it, but I signed up for the classes instead. They call that sublimating— when you do something good instead of what you really feel like doing. Anyway, I knew taking courses at the university would drive him nuts. He always thinks he's so smart, never even graduated high school, but oh, he's just so smart. Now he's moved to Kentucky of all places, with that Delphinnia woman. He thinks he'll start up his own business." Aunt Casey shook her head. "I give the whole thing two months. He's too restless to stay anywhere for much longer than that." She pulled a piece of her sandwich off and some tuna landed on the table. "There's other stuff, too, other stuff I've been angry about, but—well, anyway—we'll be talking in therapy about it, I guess."

I looked up from my sandwich.

"Yeah, we're going to have a session together today, me and you—I mean, you and I." Aunt Casey stuffed the rest of her sandwich back in the plastic and took out her pack of cigarettes. She patted the bottom of the pack, pulled one out, and lit it. She took a few puffs, inhaling hard so her cheeks sucked in, and then blew the smoke out with a deep sigh.

"It's not so bad here, is it? I mean, you're doing okay, right?"

She waited a moment for an answer.

I took a swallow of my root beer and tore at the crust on my sandwich.

"You think I don't care." She flicked her ash on the ground and took another drag. "I don't blame you, but I do—I do care. I'm taking this parenting course here, you know, where they teach you how to do it right, or better, or something."

Aunt Casey got quiet and sucked on her cigarette, studying the pine trees above us. Then she shook her head and said, "I like the parenting course, I really do, but it's like they have everything all scripted out. You're supposed to say this and then when you do, I say that, which makes you say this. We're supposed to send 'I' messages. You know, like 'I don't like my floors dirty, that's why I don't want muddy shoes on my carpet,' instead of, 'Get your muddy shoes out of my living room!' 'I' messages." Aunt Casey tilted her head. "I don't think people are that predictable. I mean, look at us, you and me. I'm sitting here saying all this stuff and I bet they have all this stuff you're supposed to be saying back to me and you're not saying anything." She pitched her cigarette into the grass. "I'm going to ask them about that in my next class. What do you do when someone won't talk to you?" She stared back toward the hospital building. "What do you do when someone won't follow the script?"

Chapter 24

DR. DEANGELIS had on running shorts and a Vulcan Marathon tee shirt when we saw him that afternoon. He smelled like his soap, or aftershave, so I guessed he hadn't gone running yet. He apologized for his casual appearance and then added that he thought it was good for the patients to see that life does go on beyond the locked doors of The Cedars.

He told us to sit anywhere and called Aunt Casey, Casey, instead of Mrs. Dawsey. Aunt Casey chose the sofa and I chose my usual chair.

Aunt Casey said, "I wouldn't mind it, Miracle, if you came and sat by me."

An "I" message. I was afraid to sit on a sofa when I couldn't even tell what color it was—too dangerous.

I stayed in my seat and Aunt Casey's face turned pink. I looked down at my legs.

"Miracle"—Dr. DeAngelis sat in his chair and rolled it to the center of the room—"your aunt spoke to you.

She deserves a response. In here we respect one another, do you understand?"

I made eye contact. "Yes."

"Good."

I glanced at Aunt Casey. "It's not you," I said, then looked down at my legs again.

"Huh? I mean, excuse me, Miracle, I didn't hear you right—ah, correctly—I don't think."

"It's not you," I repeated. "I just don't want to sit on the couch," I said to the windows just beyond her head. Dr. DeAngelis couldn't see where my eyes were.

"You don't like the couch," he said.

"No."

"Why is that?"

"What color is it?"

Dr. DeAngelis studied the sofa. "It's a very dark green, almost black."

Aunt Casey examined the armrest. "No, I don't think so, I think it's a deep navy."

Dr. DeAngelis returned to me. "What color do you want it to be?"

"A color I know."

"What does that mean? You don't want fuchsia or magenta, you want blue or brown?"

"I want one I know the meaning of, so I know what I'm sitting on."

"I don't understand," Dr. DeAngelis said.

Aunt Casey leaned forward toward me.

I said, "Red for fire or rage, purple for the highest spiritual contemplation, green for deceit and envy, yellow for the intellect."

"You're sitting on a black chair. What's black?"

"Evil, darkness, death."

Dr. DeAngelis straightened in his seat and rotated his shoulders as if he were warming up for his run.

"Where did you learn this—about colors?"

"Gigi," Aunt Casey and I said at the same time.

"Yes, that's right." He nodded, remembering. "The purple. You're wearing purple because . . . ?"

"It's the spiritual color."

"And you want spirituality? What does that mean? You want to be in touch with God or . . ."

Aunt Casey laughed. "Gigi wouldn't teach her that."

"Why do you wear purple? For Gigi?"

I shifted my gaze to his poster—THE MIND SET FREE. I tried to think. There was a reason—beyond Gigi. There was something I wanted, something important. I couldn't remember. My hands felt cold. I rubbed them. My feet were cold—my chest. I started to shiver. I held onto my chair, keeping my arms stiff to control it.

"Miracle? Are you all right? Do you know why you wear purple?"

I shook my head.

"I tried to get her to change, wear pink or plaid. Remember, Miracle? Remember that first month you were with us, I told you you didn't have to wear purple anymore?"

"Yes, I remember." The cold started slipping away, like the mercury in a thermometer—sliding off my arms and hands, down my chest, out my feet. I let go of my chair.

"Let's talk about that," Dr. DeAngelis said, pushing his heels into the carpet so his chair rolled forward closer to me.

"Let's talk about your move to your aunt's house. What was your life like living with your aunt and uncle? What do you remember most?"

Aunt Casey flopped back in her seat and folded her arms in front of her chest, waiting.

"I remember the wig heads."

"The wig heads?" Aunt Casey sat up, unfolding her arms. She looked at Dr. DeAngelis. "I fit wigs for cancer patients. I store them on plastic heads. I keep them on the shelves in her bedroom."

Dr. DeAngelis spoke to me. "What do you remember about the wig heads?"

"They watched me. They wouldn't leave me alone."

Aunt Casey and Dr. DeAngelis exchanged glances.

"They bothered you?" he asked.

"Yes."

"Did they speak to you?"

I shrugged. "Maybe, I don't remember. They didn't have any faces."

"And you wanted them to have faces?"

"Everyone should have a face, shouldn't they?"

"Do you have a face, Miracle?"

"I don't know."

"You feel maybe you don't?"

"Maybe." I looked down at his feet—so huge.

Dr. DeAngelis cleared his throat, and I lifted my head back up.

"If you don't have a face, then you're like those wig heads, aren't you?"

"Yes. Yes!"

"Is that what you're afraid of, that you're just like those wig heads?"

"I am. Yes, just like those wig heads."

"And that frightens you?"

Aunt Casey leaned forward in her seat.

"Yes. They sat on that shelf waiting."

Dr. DeAngelis rolled forward a little, and I pushed my back against my seat.

"And you were waiting, too, just like them. What were you waiting for? Do you know, Miracle?"

I tried to remember. I was waiting for something. I wore purple. I had a plan. What was my plan? I couldn't remember.

"I don't know," I said, and my own voice sounded far away.

"But you were waiting?"

"Yes. Yes, I know I was—maybe." Both our voices sounded so far away. I watched Dr. DeAngelis's face. Had he noticed?

"How else were you like those heads? Any other way?"

"They were dead."

"Do you feel dead?"

"Dead hair, dead heads."

"Miracle, look at me. Do you feel dead?"

Why did he keep trying to get me to remember? I didn't know. Something was dead. Something about me was dead, but I couldn't remember. I closed my eyes. My hands were cold again, my feet, my chest—cold spots.

A sentence came to me, popped into my head. "If

your mama was dead when you were born, then you was never born."

Aunt Casey jumped up. "Miracle! Where on earth?" She stood facing me, blocking my view of Dr. De-Angelis. I hadn't realized I had spoken out loud, but I knew by Aunt Casey's reaction that I had. I blinked at her, wondering what I had said.

I tried to think. What was it? Then I remembered and said it again. "If your mama was dead when you were born, then you was never born."

"Casey, I need to ask you to sit down," Dr. DeAngelis said. He turned his chair so it faced her way a little bit more. I rubbed my arms. They were so cold.

"Do you understand what she's saying?"

Aunt Casey nodded and tears were in her eyes ready to spill out. I wondered what I had said. What did it mean?

"Her mother was—was killed. She was hit by an ambulance when she was crossing the street."

Dr. DeAngelis nodded. "Yes, you mentioned that to me but..."

"I didn't tell you that she was pregnant with Miracle at the time."

I leaned forward, trying to hear better. Aunt Casey's voice sounded as if I were listening to it at the end of a long tunnel. I closed my eyes again and I saw a woman, in my mind, delicate looking, with freckles, standing on an iron gate.

"Miracle? Did you know this? Miracle?"

I wanted to respond, but there was that woman, I didn't want to lose her. I needed to keep my eyes closed and see her.

"Sure she knew it. Gigi must have mentioned it a hundred times a day. Thing was, I don't think Miracle liked hearing about it so much after a while. I think it made her feel like she was weird, not like the other kids. She told me once the kids teased her at school. She said she was glad to be moving to Atlanta with Opal because they teased her."

Aunt Casey's voice was breaking in, getting louder again, disturbing my picture.

"Struck by an ambulance? Did they have the siren going?" Dr. DeAngelis asked.

I opened my eyes, let go of the woman at the gate.

"Oh, sure." Aunt Casey crossed her legs and started swinging the top one. Then she saw what she was doing and stopped. "It wasn't the ambulance's fault or anything. No, we never thought that. I mean they did everything right, the siren and all, and the road was clear, no traffic or anything. Just Sissy crossing the street."

Dr. DeAngelis nodded. "An accident."

"Of course it was an accident, what do you think?" Aunt Casey flailed her arms. "Of course it was. Of course."

"You think she didn't hear the siren, or see it coming, then."

"Of course she didn't, or she'd be here, wouldn't she?"

"Would she?" Dr. DeAngelis looked out the window past Aunt Casey, as if he were trying to see the accident, see how it was. I looked through the window, too. I tried to see what he was seeing.

"What are you trying to say? That she did it on purpose?"

Dr. DeAngelis brought his focus back to my aunt and so did I.

"I didn't know Miracle's mother. I don't know the circumstances."

"You're trained to see everything as a suicide. Sheesh, that's what you do here. Work with suicides. Of course you'd think that's what happened."

Dr. DeAngelis nodded. "Yes, I do work with suicide patients and one of my patients is your niece. I'm sure you've studied enough psychology to know that suicide often runs in the family. It's the family's learned response to trouble."

Aunt Casey waved her hand. "Oh, we never told Miracle. We didn't tell her anything. Did we, Miracle? Tell him. You never knew a thing. It was just a suspicion anyway. We could never know for sure. We made a pact, we'd never tell. Gigi said for us to make her death a good thing and it was, we have Miracle." Aunt Casey glanced at me. "Gigi chose her name—Miracle. That's why she talked about Miracle's birth so much. She wanted to make it grand, glorious, a miracle. And it was, wasn't it? It wasn't a lie. That wasn't a lie."

Dr. DeAngelis shook his head. "It's a funny thing about children. The very thing adults try so hard to keep secret is the very thing they'll act out."

Chapter 25

M IRACLE, what do you think? How do you feel about what you're hearing?"

Dr. DeAngelis was watching me, wanting a reaction.

I wouldn't react to made-up stories. They were acting, putting on a show, just like in the TV room. I didn't know this woman they were talking about.

"Miracle, eye contact, please."

I wouldn't look at lies. I held my head down, tore at a fingernail.

"I'm sorry, Miracle," Aunt Casey said, sitting on the edge of her seat and leaning forward, trying to place herself in my view. "We didn't want you to get the wrong idea. We..."

"Stop talking about it!" I twisted away and covered my ears.

"You don't like what you're hearing," Dr. DeAngelis said.

"No! It's lies. Gigi could tell you. You're making everything up!"

"All right, Miracle. You may be right, but what if this were a story you read in a book and there was a young lady such as yourself, fourteen years old and..."

"I'm thirteen." I turned around to face him and brought my hands down from my ears.

Aunt Casey said, "You turned fourteen while you were in the hospital, Miracle. It's almost May now.

She was confusing me. They both were. Telling me lies and making up birthdays.

"Let's get back to the story, Miracle. An adolescent girl discovers her mother dashed in front of an ambulance while she was pregnant with her. What do you think that discovery would mean to that girl? What would it say to her? How would she feel?"

"Nothing! It's nothing. I don't have a mother. I'm nobody, who are you?" I stood up and Dr. DeAngelis held up his hands.

"All right, Miracle. It's all right. We'll leave it for now."

They gave me more pills to take at the nurses' station, to calm me down. They waited, watching me while I took them. They made me open my mouth and show them that they were gone. I didn't want to sleep. I didn't want to go to my room with all its shadows. I wanted to be in the sun, sit in bright light. The lighting was poor in the yellow unit. It was dull lighting, dull and somber. I think they used it to keep us all in a stupor. I sat in group that evening, staring through the gloomy haze, watching Leah sliding her bandage back and forth on her wrist and a boy named Rodger tilting his head from side to side, side to side, and all the voices were so far away. Mike's voice couldn't carry through the gloom. I saw him looking at me. He must have asked me a question. Everyone was looking at me. I couldn't hear them, almost couldn't see them. I needed to get nearer the light. There were too many shadows—too much danger. I stood up on the sofa and tried to climb on its back, but Kyla pulled me down. Then Joe came out of the nurses' station and they took me to my room. They moved strangely, in slow motion, and they opened and closed their mouths but no sound came out. It was like watching Aunt Casey and Uncle Toole through the window, their mouths both going at once and I couldn't hear what they were saying.

Kyla stood watch in the doorway. I sat on my bed, huddled up close to the window, my face pressed into the metal cage they had across it. I searched for the sun. The shadows were behind me. I stayed with my face pressed to the window all during group and during the dinner hour and game time. I stayed there as long as there was light. The light calmed me. I could hear sounds behind me. I heard Kyla leave. I heard Leah arguing with Joe about how many points she had. I heard Rodger teaching Deborah how to play Ping-Pong, and I could tell by the singsong tone of Deborah's voice that she was more interested in Rodger than in Ping-Pong.

Deborah came in at bedtime, five minutes till lights-out. She picked my schoolbooks up off the floor and dumped them on my bed. One of them hit me and I turned around.

"You're losing us points in here. Keep it neat."

Deborah looked angry. Her pretty blue eyes were dark; they looked almost black, evil.

I grabbed the books up in my arms and left the room. Marla, the night nurse, was on duty. She scooted out from behind her glass windows, pointing her finger at me.

"No you don't. It's time for lights-out."

"I can't sleep tonight."

The nurse turned back toward her office. "Let's see what meds you're on."

"No. No. I won't sleep. I need to be in the light. Please let me stay out here. I'll be good—I'll behave." I stepped over the red tape into the center of the dayroom. "I won't step over the red tape. I'll, I'll read." I held up my books. "See, I have this book here, these poems."

Marla went into her office and picked up the phone. I watched her through the glass, her mouth moving, no sound. I saw her nodding. Then she put down the receiver and came back out to me.

"Okay, fine. Any trouble though..."

I sat down in the big cushioned plastic chair that squeaked and groaned every time I moved. The cushion made my legs sweat. There was a lamp glued to the table beside it with a tiny metal cage around the lightbulb. They put cages around and over anything glass on the yellow unit. I switched on the lamp and leaned forward into its light. Marla watched me. She waited until I opened my book and started reading. Then she lifted her bell and shook it, calling "Lights-out!" She went around to all the rooms for the first check of the night, boys to the left of the dayroom and girls to the right, and then returned to her office, setting the bell down with one last clink.

I read my poems. Page after page of beautiful words and thoughts and truths—*the truest, realest things I know.*

I read

> To die—*without the Dying*
> And live—*without the Life*
> This is the hardest Miracle
> Propounded to Belief.

Emily Dickinson was speaking to me, using my name, speaking my life. I felt safe in her words, far from the shadows and the things hidden there. Her words brought me to a memory, Grandaddy Opal's basement. I was dancing to beautiful music. I remembered Miss Emmaline singing. Her beautiful voice singing such words, words I wanted for myself, and so I danced. That was real. I could feel it—inside, and I decided that night, reading poetry beneath a caged lightbulb, that real was when you could feel your whole body light up from within. When it didn't matter about day or night, dark or light, because you could carry the light with you, in the dancing, in the music, in the poetry.

I closed my eyes and the light was still there, the light from Emily Dickinson's words.

I was in my own bed when I opened them again. It was morning and Kyla was slapping her sandaled feet past the doors, ringing the wake-up bell. I lifted my head and squinted at the light shining through the window. I reached down and felt my legs the way I did every morning, reaching under the bandages and feeling the scars. Real scars—hot, swollen scars. Another memory flashed through my mind. I was dancing again. It was wild dancing. I was everywhere, diving for the floor, racing for the walls, spinning, leaping, crashing. And every crash, every dive, left a mark. I could feel it, and the next day, I could see it. They called them black-and-blue, but they were every shade, purple and red and greenish blue and then yellow and brown—all the colors. I rolled over and hung my head over the edge of the bed. My books were stacked on the floor with the poetry book on top. I reached out and placed my hand on the book and thought maybe someday I wouldn't need the bruises or the scars anymore. Maybe someday it would be all right for the scars to go away.

Chapter 26

I DIDN'T SEE Dr. DeAngelis that day. I went back to the surgery part of the hospital to have my legs examined by my doctor. He told me I was through with the dressings but to continue smearing silver sulfadiazine on them—the goop. I wore shorts for the first time since my stay in the hospital. Everyone crowded around me in group, wanting to see, asking me if my legs hurt. Leah called me lumpy-legs, and I told her to hush her mouth. Everybody except the counselors clapped. Leah was angry because they didn't take away any points from me for speaking out of turn. She said they were playing favorites, and when group was over she whispered to me, "I'll get you. Just don't turn your back."

Aunt Casey was already in the room when Kyla brought me down the hall to see Dr. DeAngelis the next day. She had a wad of tissues in her hands and was sitting in the chair closest to Dr. DeAngelis's desk.

Dr. DeAngelis stood up when I entered his room and told me to take a seat. He was wearing the same thing he had worn the first time I saw him—shirt, tie, jeans, and running shoes. His sleeves were rolled up this time, though, and he'd already loosened his tie some. I guessed it had something to do with his conversation with Aunt Casey.

I chose a different chair. I chose the plastic cushioned one, like the one in our dayroom only this one was black and looked new, no cracked plastic taking jabs at your sweaty legs.

"Well, Miracle, I hear you're doing better in group." Dr. DeAngelis sat back in his chair and rolled himself out between Aunt Casey and me, making sure he wasn't blocking our view of each other.

I didn't have anything to say to his comment so I studied his poster again: THE MIND SET FREE.

Aunt Casey blew her nose and sniffed.

Dr. DeAngelis reached back for a pen and his notepad and then smiled at me. He had big teeth. "I thought today, Miracle, we'd play the game 'I Recall.' It's quite easy. What I want you to do is think back to a memory you have, any memory, tell us a little bit about it, and then your aunt will bring up a memory of her own, triggered by yours. You understand? Then it will be your turn again, and your response will be based on something your aunt has said."

He looked at the both of us, first me, then Aunt Casey, then me again. "Any questions?"

"Can I pass?" I asked.

Dr. DeAngelis laughed. "No, I'm afraid not." He flipped in his notepad to a clean page and said, "Now, why don't we start?"

I tried to think of something that would stump Aunt

Casey, block her so she wouldn't bring up anything I didn't want to hear.

"Well—I remember being the love magician in school. I made up love potions and cast spells on the boys. All the girls wanted me to do a spell for them."

Aunt Casey cocked her head. "Miracle! When?"

Dr. DeAngelis held up his hand. "No. No questions. Not now."

"Right." Aunt Casey closed her eyes a second, then opened them and said, "I remember being in love with Toole Dawsey. We had this dream that I was going to be a beautician and get so popular and rich we'd move to Hollywood and I'd be the hairdresser to the stars. He wanted to be an actor, like Sylvester Stallone." She looked at Dr. DeAngelis. "We were real young then."

He nodded and turned to me.

"Uh—I remember Uncle Toole hanging me upside down by my ankles every time he came to see me. I didn't like it. He scared me. He's so—so bulky, and he's got this scar." I reached down and felt my own scars.

Aunt Casey smiled. "Yeah, I remember that." She caught Dr. DeAngelis's eye. "Oh, my turn. I remember—I remember Toole lighting firecrackers in the back of our house. It wasn't even the Fourth of July, but he loved explosives. Anything with noise. I remember one exploding and almost taking his head off. He's got thirty-two stitches in his forehead."

They had this game planned. They were trying to lead me to my legs. Dr. DeAngelis wanted me to say what happened, only I didn't know what happened. I tried to steer the game away from scars.

"I remember getting banged up in dance. I love

to dance. Dancing is real. When I dance, everything I feel comes out. I used to dance all day long at—at Grandaddy Opal's. I'd dance on the furniture and his *National Geographics*. I used to imagine—I used to imagine that someday I'd be able to step out of all my purple and dance and everyone would see me, they'd understand. I thought if they could just watch me dance they'd know all my feelings. I wouldn't have to say anything. If they could have just watched me. Nobody ever watched me."

Aunt Casey and Dr. DeAngelis exchanged a look. I didn't know what it meant. Aunt Casey sat up in her chair and took a deep breath.

I clutched the edge of my chair and wondered how she was going to bring what I said back to scars. If she did, I was going to call cheating.

"I—I remember the first time Sissy, your mama, saw dance. A dance company came to the school, some ballet company. When she got home—she was maybe seven—she couldn't stop talking about it. She said she was going to be a ballerina when she grew up. My parents thought she'd forget about it after a few days, but she didn't. She started dancing all over the house—stupid stuff, you know, little kid stuff. Finally my parents signed her up for lessons and she did it, she became a ballerina."

I didn't say anything at first. My hands were gripping the sides of my chair so hard they were starting to cramp. Then I spoke, cautiously, as though I were testing the temperature of the bathwater with my toe. "I remember—we had recitals every year when I took dance lessons, but—I was never in them because they were late at night and nobody was supposed to know about the lessons. Anyway—anyway, no one would have come so..."

"Sissy loved recitals. She loved performing. She danced all year long, even in the summer. There was this summer program at the beach one year, at the arts academy there. Sissy wanted to go so badly, but Mama and Daddy had died in a plane crash. Daddy loved to fly. He had his own plane at Eldrich Field. He was taking Mama up for a birthday ride, showing her some new things he'd learned, and this storm just came out of nowhere. After that, it was just the two of us. Sissy wasn't sure she should leave me, but I knew she needed to go. We used some of Daddy's insurance money to pay her way."

I sat with my mouth dropped open. I didn't know this. I didn't know any of it. Why didn't I know about Mama? Why didn't anyone ever tell me anything about her life? I glanced at Dr. DeAngelis. He was tapping his pen against his notepad. I looked at Aunt Casey. Was it safe to go on? Were they going to start lying again like last time?

"Miracle, it's your turn," Dr. DeAngelis said.

"When—when I danced—sometimes it felt like flying. I used to think maybe I could be a dancer and Gigi would take me to a beach house and make me tuna and tomato sandwiches while I danced and danced and danced."

"Sissy met your father at the beach that summer. He saw one of her performances. They used to have to sneak out at night to meet each other because the academy had strict rules about curfew and Gigi, well, Gigi expected Dane to be chained to his chair day and night, writing."

"No!" I pushed back in my chair. "Game's over."

"Do you remember something, Miracle?" Dr. De-Angelis asked in his soft voice. "Something about Dane, your father. Do you remember Dane?"

"No! No Dane! You're cheating. I don't know anything. I don't want to know about him."

"It's all right. You're safe here. It's safe to remember him here."

"No, it's dangerous. It's dark. You're pushing me off. You're pushing me. Don't say his name again."

"Miracle, slow down. Let's slow down."

I reached for a poem—a line, any line. I needed to feel that light inside. "They make us walk backwards, so we can see where we have been."

"Miracle?"

"Amazing grace how sweet the sound." I stood up and ran to the window.

"Miracle. You're safe. Nothing's happening. Look at the floor. It's still there. The chairs are where they've always been. Look outside. Another sunny day. There's that pine tree, same old tree. There's the blue unit across the quadrangle. It's all there. You're safe, and you know what I know about the dark? Miracle. There's always light after the dark. You have to go through that dark place to get to it, but it's there, waiting for you. It's like riding on a train through a dark tunnel. If you get so scared you jump off in the middle of the ride, then you're there, in the tunnel, stuck in the dark. You have to ride the train all the way to the end of the ride.

There's the light. It's waiting for you, Miracle. Don't jump off in the middle."

"No, I already have the light." I pressed my face to the window. His window didn't have a cage.

I heard Dr. DeAngelis stand up. He took a few steps toward me. "You're very upset. Can you tell me about it? Miracle? Were you surprised to find out your mother was a dancer?"

I turned from the window.

"You didn't know that, did you?"

"Nobody told me. Why didn't I know? How come no one ever told me about Mama?"

"Come sit down and let your aunt tell you about it."

"I—I had to keep my dancing a secret. Every time I walked home from class I had to race over the sidewalk because that big eraser was coming up behind me, erasing the lesson. I'd just make it, leaping over the cracks in the sidewalk with that eraser erasing the very square I'd just leaped from."

"You must have been very frightened." Dr. DeAngelis backed up and sat in his chair. He gestured for me to go to mine. I took the one in the corner with the silver legs.

"When Gigi found out about my lessons, she was so angry." I lifted my head up and asked Aunt Casey, "Why was she so mad? Why didn't she want me to take lessons?"

"Miracle"—Aunt Casey scratched her nose—"your mama loved dance so much, like you. She had such big dreams. She wanted to go to New York after that summer. She was sixteen, it was time, but she met—she got pregnant. She didn't even know at first. She was so skinny even when she was eight months pregnant she looked the same, just this basketball where her belly used to be. She was four months pregnant before she even realized something was different. I was the one who noticed it."

I closed my eyes and leaned my head against the wall. This was just a story. Aunt Casey was just telling me a fairy story.

"She was back at home. I was taking care of her. See that was the thing. Sixteen years old, she was still a baby herself. She lived at the dance studio. She didn't know anything about life, taking care of a baby. She still slept with all her stuffties—Pooh Bear and Ernie and Fluff Fluff—she had about twenty of them. When I'd go to her bed to wake her up in the morning, I could hardly find her she was so buried under all those animals."

Aunt Casey stopped speaking. I opened my eyes. Was it over? Was that the end of the story?

Aunt Casey reached for another tissue from the box on the desk. Her hand was trembling. She wiped her forehead and the tissue fluttered like a nervous moth in her hands. She spoke again.

"It was getting hard waking her up in the mornings. That was the first thing I noticed. She was always such a cheerful morning person, never needed coffee to get her going. Then, of course, her belly was swollen. She said she had so much gas, she couldn't get rid of it. Over-the-counter pills didn't work so I took her to the doctor. She told us Sissy was pregnant."

Aunt Casey looked at me with this pleading expression on her face, asking me to understand, but I didn't. It was just a story. It had nothing to do with me.

"See, Miracle, she couldn't give up her dream. I tried to make her see that she had a baby to think of now. I found out who the father was, found his number, and called him. I got Gigi. Then Gigi just took over. She arranged for them to live with her. They rented a house near my house with some of Da—of the father's writing money, and Sissy moved in with them.

"It was pure torture for Sissy. She and—and the father, well, they didn't get along at all. They were two selfish egos living in the same house. Both of them were spoiled babies. Both of them needed someone to take care of them. Gigi did. She smothered them with her care, made Sissy take naps, wouldn't let her dance, made her eat special macrobiotic foods. It was killing Sissy. She felt trapped. She used to call me on the telephone every day, crying about how she just wanted to dance. That's all, just dance. She would die if she couldn't dance. Then one day she called me and she was all agitated—nervous. She said she had come to a decision. She was going to have the baby, leave it with Gigi and the uh, father, and then take off for New York. She was going to be a dancer. She didn't know how to take care of a baby. She didn't want it—she didn't know the baby then, see. It was just something weighing her down. She didn't think of it as a human being or anything. She was just thinking about herself. That's all she ever had to think of—herself, her dance."

Aunt Casey tossed her wad of tissues toward the

garbage can on the other side of Dr. DeAngelis's desk. She missed. I stared at the wad and let Aunt Casey's words float over me.

"I tried to talk some sense into her. I told her how Mama and Daddy had sacrificed for her, for her dancing, it cost so much, lessons of every kind, costumes, new ballet shoes and slippers every week. It was time she learned to make some sacrifices, too. And I remember she said, 'But don't you see, all Mama and Daddy's sacrifices would have been for nothing if I don't dance. It's not like other careers. This is my prime. If I don't dance now, I don't get another chance a few years down the road.' "

Aunt Casey lowered her head and hunched forward over her lap. I waited for her to go on. She didn't say anything for the longest time. I looked to Dr. DeAngelis to do something, say something, but he just sat back in his chair looking as if he were waiting for a bus and had all the time in the world. When Aunt Casey lifted her head again she had tears on her face. She grabbed some more of Dr. DeAngelis's tissues.

"I made her feel so guilty. I told her it was her own fault she was pregnant. I said she had to start taking some responsibility for her own actions for a change. I said everything wrong—I guess." She glanced at Dr. DeAngelis. "I just didn't want the baby to grow up without a mother, without the love we had had. And then what happened?" Aunt Casey looked at me over the tissues she had pinched to her nose. "That baby grew up without her mother, without love."

I looked at the two of them. They were both staring at me as if it were my turn to say something. What did

214

they want me to say? Why were they looking at me? What did that baby have to do with me?

"What?" I said. "What do you want?"

Dr. DeAngelis spoke. "You know the rest of the story, Miracle. Why don't you tell us what happened next?"

they weren't me to say? Why were they looking at me?

What did that baby have to do with me?

"What," I said. "What do you want?"

Dr. DeAngelis spoke. "You know the rest of the story, Miracle. Why don't you tell me what happened next?"

Chapter 27

"M IRACLE? The ride's not over. Don't hop off now, we're still in the tunnel." Dr. DeAngelis rolled his chair toward me. I hated feeling cornered. I stood up and went back to the plastic chair.

"Stop looking at me," I said, adjusting my legs so the goop wouldn't stick to the seat.

"You know what happened to Sissy next."

"No, I told you I don't know it. I don't."

Dr. DeAngelis wheeled his chair to my new seat and sat in front of me, waiting. He didn't say anything. I glanced at Aunt Casey. She was bent over her tissues, staring at them, sniffing.

The room was quiet. I hated the silence. All kinds of thoughts could pop up in that silence. Silence was like the dark, anything could be hiding in it.

"I don't know," I began. "Maybe—maybe Sissy didn't run off to New York." I looked up. Still that silence. "Maybe—" I stopped. I lowered my head and closed my eyes. I could see a picture—a scene in my mind's eye, a familiar scene. It was the same one that flashed in my mind every time Gigi told me the story of my birth. Yes, I hated when she told me that story. Something was always wrong with it. She always told it the same way. Mama hurrying across the street. Mama too big to move fast enough, to get out of the way. Mama getting hit by the ambulance. The doctors pulling me out of Mama's dead body, a miracle, full of omens and portents. She said it the same way every time, and every time a scene of how it was flashed across my mind, and the picture, that scene, was never the same as her words. They never matched. Until then, I had never noticed that. I saw Mama sad, the way she was in the picture of her on the iron gate. I saw her standing on the side of the street looking down the road to check for traffic. I saw her watching the ambulance, waiting for it to pass, its siren screaming, blocking out her own thoughts, her ability to reason, there wasn't time. There was just the screaming siren, the speeding truck, there was no time to think, she just did it, she stepped out in front of the ambulance. She let it hit her. I saw it. I knew how it was. I had always known. I had always known!

I opened my eyes and looked at Aunt Casey.

"I knew," I said, reaching down along my legs, feeling for my scars.

"What?"

Tears filled my eyes. I blinked, and they ran down my face. "I knew about Mama! I always knew. I don't know how but..."

"Your family told you, Miracle," Dr. DeAngelis said, rolling in closer, leaning forward.

Aunt Casey stood up and came over to where we were. "No, we never did. We didn't want her to ever feel she wasn't wanted."

Dr. DeAngelis nodded. "Yes, the family secret, one you had to guard so closely that you couldn't be near Miracle, couldn't get too close to her or she might find out, and she could never find out."

Aunt Casey squatted down next to me. "Yes. Yes, I see that." She placed her hand on my arm. "Miracle."

I let her keep it there.

"But then how did she know?" Aunt Casey turned her face to Dr. DeAngelis. "If we didn't tell her, how did she know?"

"But you did, all of you did." Dr. DeAngelis flipped through his notes as if the words he was saying were in them somewhere. "She could read the truth in your actions, your gestures, your words, even the words that were left out. Her mind simply filled in the blanks."

Dr. DeAngelis let me go. He wanted to give me time to think, to remember. He said the two of us would work together for a while, work through the memories, fill in the rest of the gaps. He had patted my shoulder, said I'd done an excellent job. He was proud of me. I had gone through the first tunnel. Before I left the room he handed me a notebook. The pages were blank. He said I was going to write my life's story in it. He said he had more if I needed it. He wanted me to write down everything I could remember, everything important to me. He said he'd help me work through some of the issues my writings brought out. Then he said I could go. I needed time to think.

I left Dr. DeAngelis's room, and Aunt Casey came

with me. We walked down the hall together and then, before we reached the end where it opened out into the dayroom, she grabbed my arm. "Wait, Miracle," she said. "I need to tell you—I want to tell you how it was for me." She glanced toward the dayroom, then turned back to me. "See, Gigi was right. That day when we were fighting over you in the wheelchair, she said I didn't care about you. She said I was just feeling guilty, that it was all my fault. I was—I do feel guilty. Sissy was my responsibility. I gave her no other choice but to do what she did. When she died I just couldn't believe it. I couldn't accept what had happened, that it had anything to do with me. I used to come over to your house for séances, remember?"

My body shivered. I turned away from Aunt Casey but she drew closer, hemming me in, forcing my back against the wall.

"I needed to talk to Sissy. I needed to know it was all right, that she was okay, you know? I mean, I never believed in that psychic stuff before, but I just thought maybe, if she could just tell me..."

Aunt Casey sighed and took my hand. She studied it, and I studied her face. She was biting down on her lower lip and blinking several times, quick little flutters. I thought she would cry.

She shook her head and squeezed my hand. "Your hands are just like hers, and your body—just like hers, another dancer. I knew it. By the time you were three years old, I could tell you had her body. I knew you'd be a dancer." She looked at me. "I couldn't stand it, all that guilt. Every time I saw you I felt such guilt. It was like a punishment to come for a visit, but I couldn't stay away." Aunt Casey sniffed. "I guess Dr. DeAngelis would say I needed to punish myself, so I hung around. You were my punishment. See, that's how I always saw it, you were always there to remind me of what happened to Sissy."

I didn't want to hear any more. It was too much—too much. I tried to break free of Aunt Casey, holding the notebook Dr. DeAngelis had given me up to my face.

Aunt Casey grabbed my arms and pulled them down. "No, Miracle, it's not like that now. See? It's not like that. All that guilt—I see now. I know now. You're not my punishment, you're my opportunity. See?"

"Let me go," I said.

"You're Sissy's child—her beautiful child. I have a chance to do it right. I want to, Miracle. I want to make it up to you. I want you in my life."

"Well I don't want you!" I shouted, pushing her away from me. I ran away, to my room. I shut the door and leaned against it, panting and staring down at the notebook in my hand. I opened it. So many blank pages, like silence, like the dark, so many pages to fill to keep the evil away. I closed the book, closed it on my thoughts and memories and stashed it under my pillow. I left the room and went to watch television.

Chapter 28

I DIDN'T THINK ABOUT anything all day. I watched the television, ate my meals, participated in group, fought with Leah, who gave me another warning, played Ping-Pong with Deborah because Rodger was on restriction and couldn't cross over the red tape, and I read my poems.

That night, though, after lights-out, I couldn't push down the memories any longer. I stared out at the shadows from beneath my blankets and heard Aunt Casey's voice speaking in my head: "It wasn't an accident—she didn't want the baby—she loved to dance—Sissy was a dancer—you have her hands, her body."

Sissy, my mother, was a dancer. An old memory flashed through my mind. I saw Gigi's stricken face the day of the tornado when I had danced for her. I realized she didn't want me to dance because she was afraid I would end up like Sissy, but she couldn't stop me; I did end up like her. It was just as Dr. DeAngelis had said, the very thing they tried to keep secret was the very thing I had acted out. But I was still alive; I wasn't Mama. Aunt Casey needed to know that. I needed to tell her, I wasn't Mama. She was a dancer, a ballet dancer. I liked modern dance better. Yes, I liked that, knowing I liked modern dance better. "I like modern dance better." I said it over and over until Deborah told me to hush. Then a new idea came to me. It slipped out from where it had been hiding, my own idea, an exciting idea. I wanted to make up dances, become a real choreographer. I wasn't Sissy at all. I reached down beneath my blankets to my legs. The scars didn't feel so hot to the touch anymore. I smiled to myself, pleased with my dream. Me, Miracle McCloy, a choreographer. No, I didn't need Sissy, or anybody. I didn't need Aunt Casey. I had my dances, and that's all I needed.

The days passed and Dr. DeAngelis and I went over and over the story about Mama's death the same way Gigi used to do, only we told the truth, and Dr. De-Angelis made me think about the baby in the story—me, what it was like for her. What did it feel like to be her? How did it feel? How did it feel? Every question Dr. DeAngelis asked was how did it feel, or how did I feel, and how do I feel now?

I didn't know I had so many feelings. I didn't know there were so many words to describe all of them.

Aunt Casey came to most of my sessions. I told her she didn't need to come to any of them, but she came anyway. She said she wasn't going to give up. She said we belonged together. Wherever I sat in Dr. DeAngelis's room, she pulled up a chair next to me and held my hand.

When Dr. DeAngelis had me tell her my feelings,

what it was like living with her and Uncle Toole, I did. I told her exactly what it was like, but she didn't leave when I told her. She didn't leave when I cried. She just squeezed my hand and cried, too.

In every session, Dr. DeAngelis asked me if I had started writing in my notebook yet, and each time I told him that I hadn't.

What was holding me back, he wanted to know. What was still there waiting for me to face? Why was it safer for me to bury what I knew, tell myself I didn't know? I could face it, he told me. I was stronger now. I could face the truth, all of it.

What about Dane? Did I remember Dane? What happened to Dane? Dr. DeAngelis wanted to know. Every session he asked me. I told him what I remembered. I told him Dane melted.

He said, "That's impossible, Miracle. I know you know that."

"No, I don't know it. He melted, that's all I know," I said, hugging myself in my purple and thinking suddenly of Gigi. Where was she? I needed to see her. I needed to get away from Dr. DeAngelis and Aunt Casey and all their questions, all their words. I had something I needed to say to Gigi, only I didn't know what. I thought if I saw her it would come to me.

Then I had a dream about Gigi. She told me to follow her, beckoning to me with her purple fingers. She led me to an empty room with no windows. We stepped inside and the door closed behind us and disappeared. We stood in total darkness. I couldn't see Gigi or her purple fingers; everything was black. I stood there a long time waiting for Gigi to tell me what to do next, but she never did. I wanted to reach out and feel for her, make sure she was still there. I wanted to say something to her so that she would answer me back, only I was afraid if I reached out, if I spoke, I would discover she wasn't there anymore, so I just stood in the dark, waiting.

That dream stayed with me all through the next day. Dr. DeAngelis brought up Dane again during our session, and I asked for Gigi. Where was she? I needed to see her.

Dr. DeAngelis ignored my questions and asked me again, "Where is Dane?"

"I told you," I said. "He melted."

Dr. DeAngelis slammed his fist on his desk, startling me. He liked doing that. He'd startle me, get me angry, confuse me, so I'd say things I didn't want to say.

"Miracle, you're fourteen. You know the difference between fact and fantasy. You know what's real and what isn't."

"I don't," I said, my voice rising, my hands in fists.

"Miracle, you know!" He pounded the desk again.

"No, I don't know! Stop telling me I know!"

"But you *do* know!"

"How should I know what's real? Ouija boards? Séances? Tell me, I want to know! What's real? Love potions, wig heads, secret dance lessons? Black holes? Melting? Which ones are real? Miracles? Are miracles real? Tell me, Dr. DeAngelis, are you real? How do you know? How do you know? Did you ever set yourself on fire to see if you were real?"

I stopped. Dr. DeAngelis was nodding. I shoved back in my chair and turned away to stare at the wall.

"Is that what happened, Miracle? Tell me about that day. Tell me about the day your legs caught on fire."

I turned my head and glared at him. "I don't remember. Stop asking what I don't remember."

"You're doing well, Miracle. It's safe here." Dr. DeAngelis's voice was soft. "You can remember. I'm here. It'll be all right. Your aunt said there were bottles with candles stuck in them. She said they belonged to Dane. Is that right?"

"No! That's wrong. They were *my* candle bottles. I earned them."

"Your aunt said..."

I jumped up from my chair. "Stop telling me what she said! Listen to what I'm saying. Stop pushing me. I don't want to go there. Where's Gigi? I want to see her."

"All right, Miracle. I'm listening. You're doing well. You've done an excellent job today."

Dr. DeAngelis said that every time I expressed my angry feelings. He said my outbursts were good for me, but all I knew was that they left me rattled and confused.

I spent the rest of the day in the TV room and nobody got after me about it. Then the next day, Gigi came to see me. She didn't come into the yellow unit. She waited for me outside and had Kyla come get me. She said she didn't want to see "that Dr. DeAngelis man." She said it the same way I always said "Mr. Eugene Wadell," as if the words had a bitter taste to them. I wondered if words had flavors the same way we have auras, and the way colors and numbers have meanings. I asked Gigi and she said, "Of course they

225

do." She had been waiting for me out under the pine trees near the picnic tables in her green robe—green, for ceremonies concerning transcendent knowledge. She began walking and I walked with her, pleased to be seeing her, to be talking the way we used to talk. And Gigi seemed happy that I had given her something to talk about.

"Words come from the belly and up through the mouth," she said. "So of course they have flavors—sweet, bitter, salty, sour. Different combinations of words create different flavors. And people can become ill if they use too much of the same flavor." Gigi was leading me out toward the parking lot. I could see her van. It looked different somehow, but I couldn't figure out why until we got a little closer; she had painted the bumpers gold.

"Word flavor is a whole big study," she said. "Some people claim you can cure cancer in a person just by getting them to speak and think the right combination of word flavors."

We had reached the van and Gigi was digging into the pocket of her robe for her keys. "Now, here we are," she said. She was breathing hard as if we had run to the van, and her hands were fumbling with the keys so much she dropped them. I picked them up for her.

"Are you leaving already?" I asked.

Gigi unlocked the passenger's door and opened it for me. "We both are. They said you could spend the day with me. Isn't that nice? I see you're still wearing your purple. It's working, too, your aura is a nice lavender shade." Gigi said all this in a rush, hurrying around to her side of the van and dropping the keys again before unlocking her door and climbing in.

I hadn't kept track of my points. I never expected to go "off grounds" with anyone. I got in the van smiling.

Gigi huffed into her seat, slammed the car door, and said, "Now then, we're off, huh?"

She started the car and zoomed back out of her parking space, slamming on the brake just before smashing into the front end of the Jaguar parked behind us. She hung her head over the steering wheel, took a deep breath, and then eased her foot off the brake. We rolled out of the lot and down the road, away from the yellow unit, the blue unit, and the hospital.

Gigi pulled out onto the highway headed north, took another deep breath, and switched on the tape already in the player. It was flute and harp music with birds and chimes in the background—one of Gigi's subliminal tapes for losing weight.

"Where are we going?" I asked, knowing that Aunt Casey's home was south, and Atlanta was west, knowing that Tennessee was north.

Gigi didn't answer. She pretended to meditate on the tape. I sat back in my seat and stared out my window, watching the people in the cars watching us. We were the freak show, our purple van with the stars and the moon and the crystal balls. I thought about the saying on the back of the van, OPEN YOUR MIND AND TRAVEL BEYOND THE UNIVERSE. Beyond the universe, that was Gigi's world—and mine. She had taken me there, taught me all the rules—about numbers and colors and incense, about contacting the dead—the same way she would teach me about word flavors and healing. That's what she was talking about in the van on our way to Tennessee. She lowered the sound on the tape and said, "I've got the healing powers now, Miracle. When we were in Greece I saw a channeler and she took me back through all my past lives and, do you know, I was a healer in all my past lives? I was even Asklepios. That's why I received all those healing dreams."

Yes, that's what I wanted to hear. "Tell me, Gigi," I said, sinking into my seat, preparing to hear her story.

Gigi turned off her weight loss tape and pressed down on the accelerator.

"I can cure you," she said. "How 'bout it? You'll be my first cure. My miracle cure! You'll be in all the papers. Everyone will come to see. Once people hear how I made all your burns just melt away, and your legs..."

My burns *melt*! No! I didn't want to hear that. I sat up in my seat. Something hard like a tooth had clamped down on my stomach. I could hear Juleen Presque's voice saying, "People see what they want to see, and don't see what they don't want to see. It's all illusions and magic tricks."

"No, I believe it. I believe!" I said, breaking into Gigi's words.

Gigi glanced at me, startled. "Of course you do, baby. What's not to believe? We'll put you on the special healing bed. Oh, and I have the perfect spell for you. And you'll go to sleep and dream the healing dream."

Gigi held her right arm up in front of her, her palm

open as if she held the healing dream in her hand, as if she were offering it to me right there. All I had to do was reach out and take it and everything would be all right again. Everything would be the way it used to be. Isn't that what I wanted? I thought I did. I thought I could get back with Gigi and we could go on as before, talking about auras and contacting the dead. I thought I wouldn't mind going to Tennessee with her. I could forget about Dr. DeAngelis and all his questions: "How do you feel about that? What does it mean to feel nothing? What happened to your mother? Where's Dane?"

I looked over at Gigi's right hand still held open for me. I wanted to reach out and take it, I wanted to believe in her, but as in the dream I had had two nights before, I couldn't, and I awoke now with a sudden flash of understanding, a knowing that part of me had stopped believing in her the day Juleen Presque had come to see me. Juleen Presque had called Gigi a phony. I remembered that. I remembered! And I remembered I was determined to prove Juleen wrong. I would show her, and the wig heads, and everyone else. Yes, I remembered. I remembered!

I had taken out the candle bottles and lit them and had stood among them waiting to melt. I wanted to prove to everyone that Gigi's world was real, that I was real. Then came that moment, the moment I had chosen to forget until then, riding in the van with Gigi as she held her world back out to me. It was the moment after the robe had caught fire and the flames seared my skin. I felt an instant of the cruelest pain, and in that instant, I saw the truth: Gigi was a phony, and Dane didn't melt. Dane didn't melt! He didn't melt!

I turned to Gigi that day in the van and said to her, "I believed you!"

Gigi's arm came down, her hand folded over the crystal dangling from the rope around her neck. "Believed me? Well of course you did, baby. What are we talking about here?"

"I believed what you said about omens and portents and miracles."

"Miracles? Of course. *You're* a miracle, born from the body of a dead woman! Of course you believe..."

"I was born from the body of a dead woman? A dead woman, Gigi! What is that? That's not Mama! You never told me about Mama. She was just a dead woman who gave birth to me. She wasn't Sissy. She wasn't a person, a dancer. You didn't want me to know she was a dancer. She was just a dead woman, a nothing! I was born from nothing! You taught me that, Gigi. Why?"

Gigi's eyes were blinking as if they were trying to signal the answer. An angry flush grew from beneath the collar of her robe, rising up her neck and spreading out over her face. "Why are you shouting at me like this? I taught you good things. You were my apprentice, remember?"

"Yes, I was your apprentice, and I believed you. I believed everything you said. I believed in the incense, and the dances around the table to ward off evil, and magic and miracles. I believed in yellow for intellectual pursuits, and green for transcendent knowledge, and purple!" I tugged at my shirt. "I especially believed in purple. Purple was spiritual. Purple would make me just like you. Purple would bring Dane back to me and make me real. I just wanted to be real."

"Dane!" Gigi put on her blinker and pulled off to the side of the road. She stopped the car. I could see tears slipping into the creases of her face. She opened the ashtray and pulled out some fresh sheets of toilet tissue to dab at her eyes.

"Have you been talking about Dane with that doctor?" she asked, twisting in her seat to face me. She glared at me, waiting for me to answer her, and I felt myself shrink, my body dissolve into its familiar nebulous state. I began to shake. I could hear Dr. DeAngelis speaking to me, asking me why it was safer to bury what I knew. Telling me to go forward, to stay on the train, look at the truth. When I was with Dr. DeAngelis, when he asked me about Dane, my mind reached out for Gigi. I had something I needed to say to her. I thought I wanted her to rescue me, take me with her to Tennessee, I thought that's what I needed to tell her, but then I realized that wasn't it at all. I wanted her to release me. I wanted her to say it was all right to stop believing. I wanted to break the unspoken pact we had kept between us for so many years.

I sat up and turned to face Gigi. Her face was still a rash of red blotches but the tears were gone. I looked in her eyes just the way Dr. DeAngelis would have wanted me to and asked, "Where's Dane?"

Gigi's mouth dropped open.

"Where's Dane? Where is he?"

Her eyes widened. She leaned back, away from me. "You know where he is."

I shook my head. "No, the truth. Where is he? What happened that night of the séance?"

"You know what happened." Gigi's hand clutched at

her crystal. "He melted, remember? You saw for your-self. You saw the candle bottles. You saw his clothes."

"No! I don't want to hear your lies. Where did he go? What happened to him? Why did he leave?"

Gigi shook her head. "I told you, Miracle, I told you he melted. That's all I know. He melted."

"Gigi!" I slid closer to her and raised the leg of my purple pants, raised it up to expose the scars. "People don't melt, they burn. See? They just burn."

Chapter 29

GIGI DIDN'T LOOK DOWN at the burns on my leg, but I did. I looked down at them as if I were seeing them for the first time, my burns, my scars, vestiges of my last desperate attempt to feel something, to feel real, to feel the truth.

I lifted my head. I wanted to tell Gigi what I was feeling, make her understand why I needed the truth.

Gigi was staring out the windshield.

"But Dane melted," she said, her voice quivering, her head tilted. She turned to me.

I looked in her eyes and I could see that she was pleading with me, asking me to believe. Begging me to keep our silent pact, to stay with her in her fantasy world. But I couldn't do it. I had realized it wasn't safe there anymore, if it had ever been. There was nothing there for me. I was nothing, felt nothing when I lived in that other world. I shook my head and started to turn away.

"He melted," Gigi said again, grabbing me with her words.

I didn't want to look at her. I didn't want her to pull me in, but I couldn't help it. I tried staring at her hands locked together in a tight grip. She had put on weight. The bracelets on her wrists pressed into her flesh. I lifted my head and Gigi looked at me, pleading. Wrinkles ran down her face like a thousand frowns. I could read her pain as if I had struck her in the chest. I could read her fear, and I nodded. I understood that fear. Gigi still needed to believe. She wasn't lying to me. She believed what she told me. She believed Dane had melted. She had to. Knowing that Dane left her because he didn't want her anymore was more than she could bear. It was the loneliest, most desperate feeling in the world. That's what I knew. That's what I would tell Dr. DeAngelis when I saw him again. When he asked me where Dane was, I would tell him he left us. He ran away. And when he asked me how it made me feel, I would tell him...my thoughts stopped. No, it wasn't just the loneliest feeling. It wasn't just the emptiness, it was—it had been, a need. All those years I needed Dane, I needed him desperately to make me feel safe and real, but what I realized, staring again at my scars, was that I was real right there, right then. I didn't need those scars anymore, I didn't need Dane or Mama to make me feel real. How did it happen? When? I studied my hands, touched my face, I was real, and it wasn't Dane or Mama who made me so, it was knowing the truth—all of it. The truth made me real.

I wanted to sing out, to dance, to move the way I

was feeling inside, wild and ecstatic, but Gigi held me back, bringing me down with her voice.

"Miracle?" Her voice pleaded once again.

I turned to face front, away from Gigi. I couldn't help her. I didn't know how. My own feelings were too new, too fresh. Thoughts and memories were slamming around inside my head, crashing into one another, exploding, breaking wide open. I needed time. I needed a chance to sort them all out. I needed someone to talk to who would understand and listen, really listen. I needed Dr. DeAngelis and Aunt Casey. I wanted to tell them everything, to share what I was discovering with them, and to let them know I needed them.

"Would you take me back to The Cedars, please?" I asked, staring straight ahead.

Gigi sat up and reached for another piece of toilet tissue. "But I'm taking you to Tennessee. I can heal you. I can send you the healing dreams." She sniffed and wiped her nose. "You'll be my first cure—my miracle cure. We'll take pictures—before and after. You'll be written up in all the papers—Miracle McCloy and the Miracle Cure."

I shook my head. "I don't want to be a miracle. I just want to be a girl. I just want to be normal." I looked at her. "Please. Take me back to The Cedars."

Gigi shook her head and the loose skin under her chin wobbled back and forth. "But I can't. They'll think I kidnapped you. That prying Dr. DeAngelis will get after me."

"But I have to go back. I need them. I need that place."

Gigi started up the car and turned on her blinker. Then she accelerated back onto the highway. I thought she would turn around at the first exit, but she didn't. She moved into the passing lane and kept going north, to Tennessee.

I sat leaning up against the door, watching the signs go by—NASHVILLE 57 MILES, NASHVILLE 52 MILES—and I remembered other trips in and out of the state of Alabama. I had never wanted to go. I hadn't wanted to leave our home and move in with Grandaddy Opal. Then, I hadn't wanted to leave Grandaddy Opal to move in with Uncle Toole and Aunt Casey, or to leave them to stay at The Cedars in the yellow unit with Dr. DeAngelis. No, I never wanted to go, they just took me. Without asking how I felt about it, they took me, and I went without saying anything, because I was a nobody. They had made me feel like a nobody.

I stared out the window, anger welling up in me. I had to go back to The Cedars. I couldn't let Gigi take me away again.

I turned to Gigi. "Gigi, I have to go back. You need to turn around, now!"

Gigi turned on her weight loss tape and accelerated to seventy-five miles an hour.

"This really is kidnapping," I said.

"Nonsense, I'm your legal guardian." She turned up the sound on her tape.

"But you're taking me against my will. Gigi?"

She stared out at the road, pretending I hadn't just spoken to her. If she weren't driving I knew she would go into a trance. That was her way. If she didn't like

236

what she was hearing, if she didn't like what was happening, she just pretended it all away.

"Is this what you did to Dane?" I said, raising my voice to be heard over the tape. "Is this how it was?"

"Dane melted," she said, still staring at the road.

"No, before—when he was thirteen and you took him away from Grandaddy Opal. This is how it was, wasn't it? He didn't want to go. He didn't want to just write all day. He wanted to be with Grandaddy Opal and ride bikes and build things, but you just took him. You took him away from Grandaddy Opal and brought him to that beach house. He didn't want to go, did he?"

"Miracle, hush!" Gigi slowed down and moved over to the traveling lane. She hummed along with the flute, but I could tell by the deep furrows in her brow and the way she tilted her head away from me that she was listening to me, listening to what she didn't want to hear.

"And he didn't want to marry Sissy, and maybe he didn't want me, but most of all he didn't want to live the life you chose for him, so he ran away. He ran off, didn't he?"

Gigi shook her head and pointed at me. "Stop telling your lies! It's that doctor brainwashing you. Don't say another word. I knew that place would damage you. Casey and her big ideas." She glanced at me. "Look at you, your aura's black. The darkest black. That's what happens when you go to those nut houses. Everyone there walks around in a black cloud."

"No! It's good there. I'm learning good things, and Aunt Casey's there with me. She holds my hand. She rides through the tunnels with me. And Dr. DeAngelis and Kyla and everybody, they talk to me and they listen and they touch me. They're giving me something I've never had before. When I'm with them, I'm somebody. When I'm with you, I'm nobody!"

"Nonsense." Gigi shook her head as if she had a fly in her hair.

I reached over and turned off her tape. "It was the same way with Dane," I said. "He had to leave. He had to run away or he'd always be a nobody, no matter how many books he wrote. Gigi, don't make me run away, too. Take me back. I need to go back."

Gigi switched the tape back on and turned it up so loud I couldn't yell over it. She pulled some more toilet tissue out of the ashtray and blew her nose.

I sat back in my seat and faced the window, but instead of watching the other cars passing by, the people staring, trying to read our van, I watched myself in the reflection of the window. It had been a long time since I had dared to look at myself, searching for Sissy's freckles. This time I didn't look for Sissy or even Dane, I just looked at myself. It was my hair, growing out from its Dane-like cut. It was my face, long and thin, my eyes blinking back at me, my mouth, my chin—me. I stared at myself a long time and sometimes the sunlight would fall on the window and take my face away, but then there it would be again, just the same, me staring out at me. I kissed my finger and pressed it on the window where my mouth appeared. I held it there and tears spilled from my eyes. I took my finger away and watched myself cry.

Gigi turned on her blinker and shot off the highway

onto the exit ramp. She shut off the music. The silence felt wonderful.

I sat up, wiping my face. "Are we in Tennessee?" I asked.

"There's a bus station here," she said. "You can just go back to that place on your own."

I turned to thank her but she held up her hand. "You've been ruined by that doctor. My healing dreams can't possibly work on you. It would be a waste of my time and energy."

We rode into town in silence. Gigi found the bus station and checked the schedule. There was a bus leaving for Birmingham in less than an hour. She didn't wait with me, and she wouldn't look at me when she said good-bye. She looked past me, at the buses shifting gears behind me.

"You'll be all right," she said.

I nodded.

"Yes, of course you will. Now, you keep wearing that purple. You want..." She stopped. Our eyes met and then she looked away again, down at her own green robe.

"Well, safe trip then. I better get going or Eugene will start wondering where I am."

She turned away, walking off in the wrong direction. She stopped, turned around, and walked past me as if I weren't even there.

Chapter 30

I SAT DOWN ON A BENCH to wait for my bus. I watched the people passing in front of me, studied their faces, their clothes, the way they walked. I had never really noticed people before, and I wondered what it meant, to see them now, as if they were newly born upon this earth, and I, too, newly born, alive, truly alive. It felt good, so good to get away from Gigi, from the hold she had on me. I felt so free and light. I just knew if I stood up and did a leap I would leap clear over the tops of the buses and the tops of the trees and I wouldn't come down for a long, long time.

I watched a man waiting in line for his turn to buy a ticket. He looked tired, shifting his weight from one leg to the other. I wished I could lend him mine, my new legs, my leaping, springing legs. I heard him order his ticket and I sprang from my seat, not to lend him my legs, but because I had just realized I had no ticket, and I had no money.

"Gigi! How could she forget?"

I twisted around, looking this way and that, looking for a solution to my problem and believing, I suppose, that the answer hovered somewhere close, if I just knew where to look. I watched several more people purchase their tickets. I stood up and walked to the ticket counter. I paced in front of it a few times listening to a man ordering his ticket to Montgomery and wishing he'd drop a few bills by accident. When the counter was empty, the woman selling the tickets called out to me from behind her window, "Can I help you?"

I stopped and moved closer, leaning into the window. "I have to get to Birmingham."

"Yes?" The woman held out her hand.

"No, I don't have any money. I—I need to get back. What can I do?"

The woman narrowed her eyes. "You a runaway?"

"I need to get back. Aunt Casey, Dr. DeAngelis, they'll be waiting for me. She'll be waiting."

"You want me to call somebody?"

"Call?" What was she saying? "Oh! Yes, yes, can I make a call? I don't have any money. My aunt, when she comes, she'll pay you back."

The woman pushed back in her seat and brought a set of keys out of her pocket. "Well, I shouldn't, but I will. I've got a daughter just about your age. I'd want someone helping her if she ever had a mind to run off. Come on in."

She unlocked the door and showed me the phone.

I dialed Aunt Casey's number and held my breath. She answered before the first ring had ended.

"Hello!" she said, her voice sounding urgent.

"Aunt Casey, it's me, Miracle."

"Miracle! It's Miracle," she said, holding her voice away from the receiver. She got back on the line. "Where are you? We've all been so worried. Are you at Gigi's?"

"No. I'm at a bus stop. I don't have any money. I want to come home. Aunt Casey, I want to come home."

"You want to come back? To me?" Aunt Casey sounded disbelieving. "You're at a bus stop? Which one? I'll come get you."

"I—I don't know, hold on." I turned to the woman behind me. "Where am I? My aunt will come pick me up."

"Here, let me." The woman took the receiver from my hands and told Aunt Casey how to get to the station, then she handed it back to me.

"Hello," I said, expecting to hear Aunt Casey's voice again.

"Girl, what you doing way out there? I come for my first visit and danged if you don't run off. A lesser feller might be plenty insulted."

I felt my heart give a leap. "I didn't run off."

"Did too."

"Did not. Gigi took me."

"Well, you had better just hurry on back is all I got to say, before I take a mind to leave."

"No, don't leave! I need—wait for me, Grandaddy."

"Girl, I'll be waiting, don't you worry. Why do you think I made sure them doctors fixed me up right?"

"Then you're all right? Your heart's okay?"

The woman behind me gave me a nudge. "Hey, that's long distance, hurry it up."

"Grandaddy, I've got to go, but you'll be there, won't you? You're all better now? You'll come visit me in the hospital?"

"I'll be here, don't you worry. Here's your aunt to say good-bye. You hurry on home, now."

"Miracle?"

"Aunt Casey, I've got to go."

"Yes, I know, I'm on my way."

"Thanks. Oh, and Aunt Casey? Thanks for wanting me to know the truth—for wanting me."

"Miracle"—Aunt Casey hesitated—"I love you."

I hung up the receiver and thanked the woman with the tickets. She winked and let me out through the door. I went back and sat on the bench to wait. I watched the people again, getting on and off buses, passing in front of me, buying their tickets. All of them looked different, wore different clothes, different colors. I looked down at my purple outfit and told myself, *I will never wear purple again*. Then I thought, *No, I won't say never. I don't want any rules. When it comes to numbers and colors, there will be no rules. I'll wear orange and red and pink and sit on that strange blue-black-green couch in Dr. DeAngelis's office. I'll sit on it with Aunt Casey and she'll take my hand and tell me again that she loves me*.

Dr. DeAngelis once said that we would be talking about love, what it means, how it feels. I told him I didn't believe in love. "You can't touch it, or see it," I had said, remembering my conversation with the wig heads. "I won't believe what I can't see."

He said, "Then believe what you feel."

I thought about that, sitting on the bench. I thought about Dane. I had so much still to figure out. I knew I

243

no longer felt so desperate to find him, and this made me wonder if I even loved him. Did he love me? I wasn't sure anymore. I still didn't know what love was, not yet. But I thought maybe it was like dance, and music, and poetry. I knew how they made me feel, how the truth made me feel: real, and lit up from the inside, and like nothing in the world could ever really hurt me. I decided love might be like that, too, because when I thought of Aunt Casey taking those parenting courses and coming to the sessions with Dr. DeAngelis, coming to talk with me, spend time with me, and when I thought of Grandaddy Opal teaching me to ride a bicycle, teaching me how to care for something outside of myself, my own special Etain, I got that same lit-up feeling.

A woman eating from a large bag of popcorn walked up and sat down next to me. She looked at me and smiled and held out her bag, offering me some of her popcorn. I reached in, took a handful, and popped a piece in my mouth. She nodded and I smiled, thinking of her kindness, of Aunt Casey and Grandaddy Opal, thinking that love might turn out to be the truest, realest thing I'll ever know.